DEATH *by* CHOCOLATE

COCO BEAN INVESTIGATES

ANNA BROOKE

Chicken House

2 Palmer Street, Frome, Somerset, BA11 1DS
www.chickenhousebooks.com

First published in the UK in 2026
Chicken House
2 Palmer Street
Frome, Somerset BA11 1DS
United Kingdom
www.chickenhousebooks.com

Chicken House/Scholastic Ireland, 89E Lagan Road, Dublin Industrial Estate,
Glasnevin, Dublin D11 HP5F, Republic of Ireland

Text © Anna Brooke 2026
Illustration © Emily Jones 2026

The moral rights of the author and illustrator have been asserted.

All rights reserved.
No part of this publication may be reproduced, transmitted, downloaded,
decompiled, reverse engineered, used to train any artificial intelligence
technologies, or stored in or introduced into any information storage and
retrieval system, in any form or by any means, whether electronic or
mechanical, now known or hereafter invented, without the express written
permission of the publisher. Subject to EU law the publisher expressly
reserves this work from the text and data mining exception.

This book is a work of fiction. Names, characters, businesses, organizations,
places, events and incidents are either the product of the author's imagination
or used in a fictitious manner. Any resemblance to actual persons,
living or dead, events or locales is purely coincidental.

For safety or quality concerns:
UK: www.chickenhousebooks.com/productinformation
EU: www.scholastic.ie/productinformation

Cover design by Mecob
Typeset by Dorchester Typesetting Group Ltd
Printed in the UK by Clays, Elcograf S.p.A

1 3 5 7 9 10 8 6 4 2

A CIP catalogue record for this book is available from the British Library.

PB ISBN 978-1-917171-30-4
eISBN 978-1-917171-31-1

For Mom, lover of stories
For Dad, the family Francophile
For Max, the chocolate gobbler
For the ghosts in our apartment
Oh, and for Belle . . . 'Woof!'

Also by Anna Brooke

Monster Bogey
Monster Stink

Prologue

It was that time of night again. That strange time around midnight, when darkness darker than the ebony sky outside descended on the empty attic room.

And the footsteps began.

Creeping ... Pacing ... Invisible.

Then, as always, came the sigh. Soft and sad.

'*Huhhhh ...*'

Though who or what had made it could not be seen ...

Whoosh!

An icy wind!

Waft!

The faintest smell of chocolate!

Donk!

A low-hanging lightbulb swinging *left-right, left-right*, then ...

Nothing!

Until . . . the transparent silhouette of a man appeared by the window, looking out over the deserted village square, rubbing his head.

Had you been under that ebony sky outside, you might have seen the dim glow of his face through the attic window. Such a sad face!

Had you been in that room, you might have noticed a tear of ectoplasm roll down his face and plop on to the floor.

You might even have seen a mouse run across the floor and straight through his feet.

But there was no reason for you to have been there. For no living person had stepped foot in Hôtel Framboise in over forty years.

And that was the way the ghost liked it.

1

Coco Bean had not wanted to MOVE HOUSE!

She'd especially not wanted to MOVE HOUSE from her bustling hometown of Burton-on-the-Bush in England, whose name she could pronounce very well, to some run-down hilltop village in France – *Mont-Lavande* – whose name was difficult to say. Coco was only twelve, but she'd already been to France on holiday a lot (and she liked it). But moving there for good? To live in a crumbling old inn called Hôtel Framboise with peeling shutters, cracked tiles, dust and cobwebs? That looked like it hadn't seen a lick of paint since Napoleon wore nappies?

No! No! AND NO!

In England, she'd had:

- Her best friends, Kate and Rose

- A nice school
- A warm, draught-free house

But – and here's the thing – she had no choice.

You see, some parents love shopping or playing cards or ballroom dancing. Some even love dangerous things like car racing or bungee jumping or knife throwing. But what Mr and Mrs Bean loved best was France: the people, the culture, the landscapes, the food, the language . . .

That's why Coco's first name was Coco (after Coco Chanel, the great French fashion designer). That's why their dog, a sweet, gold-coloured cocker spaniel, was called Belle (the French word for 'beautiful'). And that's why they'd always gone on holiday to France, devoured magazines about French life, cooked French food at home, watched French films and binged on TV programmes about renovating French châteaux, French barns, French churches and any other French building that needed a blob of cement and a new roof.

Never mind that Coco hadn't wanted to leave England and only knew a bit of French, despite her holidays and lessons at school – France was Mr and Mrs Bean's dream, so they'd gone there. Even if it had meant borrowing a lot of money from the bank to buy the tumble-down ten-room hotel on the main square that needed more work than just cement. And even if it had meant giving up their jobs – French teachers, of course – to become hotel managers, work that neither of them had done before.

'It'll be an adventure,' her parents had promised as they'd moved the first round of boxes into the cobwebby lobby, late that June.

'It'll be a disaster!' Coco had replied, watching Belle chase a mouse over the cracked tiles and noticing that there was no Wi-Fi and the phone coverage was so weak she couldn't message Kate and Rose, who were (like she should have been) still at school.

But that wasn't the worst of it for Coco.

The worst of it was . . . the boredom!

Burton-on-the-Bush had a cinema and a bowling alley and laser tag and cafes and lots of shops, including Choco-Yum-Yums, which sold her favourite chocolates (Caramel Stars: milk chocolate with a squidgy toffee middle) and gave weekend baking classes that Coco never missed. Most importantly, it had Kate and Rose.

What did the village of Mont-Lavande (which meant 'Mount Lavender', because of the lavender fields around it) have?

Here, let's take a tour:
- Boarded-up houses
- Boarded-up shops
- A village church with a graveyard

- An old castle tower behind the church
- A tiny bakery
- A cafe called Café de la Poste, because it doubled as a post office

And . . . well, that was it. Coco had explored all of that by their second day in the village – and that had been two weeks ago.

In its heyday, over forty years ago, Mont-Lavande must have looked very pretty. You could still see old rusty shop signs for things like a florist's, a grocer's, a patisserie and even a perfume-maker's. But today, it looked . . .

'Full of potential,' Coco's parents had declared.

'Sad,' Coco had replied. 'There's nothing to do except walk Belle, and I have no friends here.'

Then there was the small issue of the HAUNTING.

2

Coco woke with a start, her eyes wide and her heart thumping.

She could hear footsteps in her attic room, pacing between the wardrobe on her left and the small, circular window ahead.

'I don't believe in ghosts!' she repeated to herself, pulling her duvet tight around her chin. 'I don't believe in ghosts!'

And she didn't.

But . . .

Why was the air suddenly icy-cold?

And why did it smell like . . . chocolate? A smell she should have loved. But here? At midnight? It was creepy.

Just like that spooky SIGHING by her left ear!

'*Huhhhh . . .*'

Coco froze.

Then ... *DONK!*

She dared to look up.

Her paper lightshade was swinging *left-right, left-right*, against the cracked, grey ceiling.

What on earth was going on?

Coco threw the duvet over her head, because ... well, who wouldn't?

It was scary.

It was weird.

And she didn't like it one bit.

Funny, isn't it? How what seems frightening at night can feel silly in the morning?

When Coco woke up and saw the summer sunlight streaming through the cracks in her curtains, she thought back to the night's events and decided that she'd been wrong.

There had to be a perfectly normal explanation for what she'd experienced. Just because her bedroom – with its ripped wallpaper and peeling paint – *looked* spooky, didn't mean that it *was* haunted! There were even a few things about it that were . . . *OK*. Like . . . erm . . . like the dust particles floating in the sunbeams by the window. *Yes*. They looked like dancing fairies – which was all right.

Footsteps in my room?

Just creaking floorboards, she told herself.

That icy wind? Just a draught.

That swinging lightshade? Same draught.

That sigh? Just my imagination.

And that chocolate smell? A trick of the brain. I've been missing England and my Caramel Stars, that's all. Ghosts aren't real.

'They *really* AREN'T!' she added out loud for good measure.

And with that decided, she turned her thoughts to breakfast. She was starving.

BANG!

What was that?

Coco ran to the window. She could just make out Mum and Dad standing in billows of dust in the little garden between the front door and the gate.

She threw her slippers on and ran out of the attic, down three flights of stairs, through a curious cold spot, across the box-filled lobby and – careful not to hit the antique mirror her parents had just splurged on – out of the front door.

'What's happened?'

It looked like a huge chunk of wall had fallen off the front of the building. Mum's brown hair was grey with dust and Dad's red beard looked white. Even Belle had gone a lighter shade of gold.

'Here! Quick!' said Mum, passing Coco her phone. 'Film me? This is brilliant.'

'Erm . . . is it?' said Coco. 'Why?'

'Just do it,' said Mum. 'I'll explain in a sec.'

Coco switched the phone to video and pointed it at Mum, wondering what on earth was going on.

'*E-hem.*' Mum cleared her throat and stared into the camera with an exaggerated smile. 'So, this huge slab of plaster just fell off the hotel facade –' she pointed up to the wall above the front window – 'and look what was underneath it. Ta-daaaaa!'

Through the screen, Coco saw old-fashioned writing painted on what must have been the original hotel front. You could just make out the letters '—ATIER'.

'We don't know what the first part of the word should be,' Mum continued. 'But it's made us realize there's more to Hôtel Framboise's history than we thought. It looks like an old shop sign or something.'

'Duh-duh-duuurrr. It's a mystery,' said Coco in a funny voice, pointing the camera on to herself then down at the rubble.

Belle barked, then howled a 'woo-woo-woo' sound, as if in agreement. Coco often thought her dog understood more than humans knew. That howl always sounded like she wanted to talk.

'OK, Coco! Stop the video!' cried Mum. 'I'll have to

do it again!'

'What? Why?'

'Cos your mum's going to become an influencer,' said Dad. 'We're not making silly videos for us. We're making good ones to put online.'

'An influencer?' said Coco. 'But don't you need like a million followers for that? You've only got ten, Mum.'

'Eleven . . . For now,' Mum corrected. 'I'm going to film us renovating the hotel in a video diary. Like in those TV shows about doing up French châteaux. You know . . .'

Coco knew. Those programmes were the reason she was there.

'And if we can get enough followers,' Dad added, 'we might be able to make some money while we do up the hotel. Cos, well . . .' He looked up at the shabby building. 'We have to have it open by next Easter.'

Coco knew they needed to open by Easter or they wouldn't be able to pay back that big bank loan. She also knew they needed to find more money to finish doing it up. But DIY? She couldn't imagine anyone wanting to watch her family doing that. But, hey, it was worth a try. And at least this way, they'd have to get the Wi-Fi sorted. Then she could *finally* message Kate and Rose.

Coco's stomach growled.

'What's for breakfast?' she said. 'Did you find those pains au chocolat?' There had been six in the cupboard, then suddenly zero!

'No! Sorry,' said Mum, taking her phone back. 'Your father must have eaten them *all*!' She gave Dad a look. 'Like those Nibby's chocolate balls we brought over with us from England.'

'OK, I ate the pains au chocolat,' admitted Dad, with a guilty smile. 'But I didn't touch the Nibby's . . . There's some money on the kitchen table, Coco,' he said, changing the subject. 'If you go up and get dressed, you can walk Belle to the bakery and get us a baguette.'

'Do I have to?' she cried. She really did not want to go to the bakery. She'd have to try to speak French.

'Yes. You need the practice. French school soon, remember?'

How could she forget? It wasn't just weird stuff in her bedroom that kept her awake at night.

OUCH! OUCH! OUCH!

The ghost sat rooted to the spot on the staircase. He couldn't believe it.

That girl. That green-eyed, brown-haired *brigand* who'd taken over *his* attic had jumped straight through him. On *his* stairs. TWICE!

There he'd been, minding his own business in a rather elegant sitting pose (elbow on knee, face on hand, like a Greek statue), when . . . URGH! He'd felt her emotions as she'd passed as if they were his own.

She was sad, bored and a little bit lonely. Or perhaps those were *his* feelings. He'd been sad, bored and lonely ever since he'd died.

And how had *that* happened again?

He scrunched his eyes to think.

He'd been in the . . . ?

When . . . ?

Then . . . ?

Nope. It was no good. He couldn't remember a single detail.

Anyway, how rude!

Never, in the forty-odd years since his death, had his peaceful afterlife in the Hôtel Framboise been so disrupted. That's why he'd hidden their English chocolate balls. To annoy them! Well, that, and because the chocolates – Nibby's – had smelt like plastic. Urgh!

In his day, only the finest of ingredients would have gone into making such sweet indulgences, but these days . . . He stopped himself. That wasn't the point! The point was, the family would never find them. *Not unless they can walk through cupboards like me!* he chuckled, and then walked through a cupboard before floating downstairs into his secret basement workshop to make his point.

He stretched out an arm and stroked the marble surfaces, oak shelves, copper saucepans and hand-painted blue and white wall tiles. 'Still beautiful, even after so many years.' He sighed.

Then he went to the pantry to admire his moulds and rows of porcelain pots, each painted with the names of what they'd once contained – flour, sugar, vanilla . . .

Bon sang! he howled (silently). He wanted this horrible

English family out of his home!

And he knew just the way to do it!

Adults were hard to scare, but children . . .

He'd already made some headway with his sighing and pacing, but it was time to crank things up.

Watch out, little girl! he thought. *Things are about to get* intéressantes!

Coco led Belle slowly through the square in front of the hotel, as Mum and Dad got on with their video making.

Belle made a beeline for a tree, so Coco let her off her lead while she took photos of the hotel from behind some low-hanging leaves, then another from the broken water fountain, where a little frog sat croaking in a puddle. Mum might like them for her profile page, she thought.

Belle rushed over, tail wagging like helicopter blades. The frog jumped away.

'I guess you don't care *where* you live,' said Coco, bending over to kiss Belle's long, velvety ears. They were still a bit dusty. 'As long as you're with us, you're OK!'

Belle licked her cheek, as if in agreement.

Coco wished she could say the same for herself.

The warm morning sun made the pale stone buildings of Mont-Lavande look like they were made of shortbread, and there was a delicious scent of lavender wafting in from the fields below. But oh, what she wouldn't give to swap the lonely, fragrant village for bustling Burton-on-the-Bush.

She looked at her phone. It was *Saturday*, the day she'd usually be at a Choco-Yum-Yums with Kate and Rose. She missed those baking classes, almost as much as she missed her friends. She wondered what they'd be making today. Mint choc chip cupcakes, maybe? She'd really wanted to learn how to do those.

'Come on!' She sighed, heading towards the cobbled road that led down the hill, past the church graveyard, and towards the bakery.

While Belle carried out the first of her daily number twos, Coco checked the photos she'd taken. In one there was a weird blob, like a face, in the kitchen window. She rubbed the lens on her phone. It was probably just dirt. Then Belle barked to say she'd finished, so Coco cleaned up the mess with a black poo bag and they walked on.

And then she saw the sign: BOULANGERIE.

Her heart began to hammer.

Her throat began to tighten.

Her hands began to sweat.

Uh-oh! This was it. She was going to have to speak French.

Coco was, by nature, a confident girl. The sort of person who stood up to bullies and didn't mind doing readings in front of her class. But . . . speaking French . . . ?

Help! her brain cried. *I can't remember any words.*

GRRRRR! went her stomach, which meant, 'Yes, you can. You must. There are delicious doughy baguettes in there and I'm hungry.'

Coco tied Belle's lead to a little metal ring that hung next to the shop door, and – trying to ignore her wobbly legs – stepped inside.

A bell tinkled as the door closed behind her. There, behind the counter, stood a short, curly-haired lady with a kind face. She dusted her hands off on her apron as she chatted to a boy.

'*Bonjour!*' the lady said automatically, glancing up at Coco.

The boy turned too. He looked about Coco's age, with short, dark hair, brown eyes, black glasses and olive skin.

And then Coco panicked. Because now she was going to have to speak in front of TWO French people! Her hands began to shake.

'*Qu'est-ce que je vous sers, mademoiselle?*' said the baker.

The boy stared.

'ERM . . .' Coco had NO idea what the lady had just said.

She squirmed on the spot as she tried to make a sentence in her brain. What were the words her parents had taught her?

'*Je suis . . . baguette!*' she blurted. Then immediately realized her mistake. *Je suis* meant 'I am'! She'd just announced that *she was* a baguette!

The boy burst out laughing.

The baker looked surprised.

Coco went bright pink, and pointed ferociously at the baguettes behind the counter before indicating she wanted one with her finger.

The baker smiled and handed her a baguette. '*Voilà!*'

Coco paid, then dashed out, so embarrassed that she didn't even wait for the change.

'You forgot your money!' cried the boy, in English, rushing out after her as she untied Belle with wobbling fingers. He had a French accent, but at least *his* English words were right. 'And your shopping!'

He handed her the poo bag.

Coco thought she'd die. She was so embarrassed. She wanted to hide in the Hôtel Framboise and never come out again. In less than thirty seconds, she'd said she was a baguette and left a poo bag in a bakery!

'Erm . . . that's not mine!' she lied.

'But I saw you leave it,' replied the boy, confused.

'Oh . . . erm . . . yes! I mean, *oui*. It is mine!'

She slunk off towards Café de la Poste next door, where there was a bin on the terrace, next to a couple of pit-stopping cyclists. She shoved the poo bag into the bin, then charged back up the hill with Belle, her eyes pinned firmly to the cobbled ground, pretending nothing unusual had just happened at all.

'You are that English girl at the hotel, are you not?' the boy called after her. He pronounced his 'th's like 'z's.

'Might be!' Coco said, keeping her head down.

'Wait!' he called, running to catch up. Belle immediately jumped on him, and wouldn't walk on until he'd petted her, forcing Coco to stop.

'What is your dog called?' the boy asked, scratching under Belle's ears. Belle's back leg started thumping the ground.

'Belle,' said Coco. She watched the boy for a second. His eyes were gentle. Not mocking. And he looked like the sort of person who laughed a lot. In one hand he had a bag of pastries (which Belle was now sniffing with great interest) and under his arm was what looked like a well-used notepad. Belle seemed to like him; he'd found her itchy spot, so he couldn't be all bad.

'What's your name?' Coco decided to ask.

'Louis,' he said. 'I live on the other side of the square. And you?'

'Coco...'

'Well, Coco, do not worry, you do not look like a baguette!' he said with a smile. 'I am sorry I laughed. We saw you move in. The hotel has been empty my whole life.' Then he paused. He looked like he wanted to say something else, but didn't know if he should.

'So, have you seen it yet?' he suddenly blurted.

'Seen what?' Coco asked.

'The ghost!'

Coco felt as though someone had poured cold water on her head.

'Ghost? What ghost?' she replied, trying to sound normal, but her voice was high-pitched and squeaky as memories of the 'weird stuff in the night' came flooding back.

'Well, everyone in the village says that many years ago, at the hotel...' Louis started, but broke off when he looked up at her.

She realized her mouth was open and her eyes were wide. She closed her mouth fast and forced a blink. But she could tell from Louis's expression that he'd seen her shocked face.

'Oh... it is nothing,' he said, suddenly changing his mind. 'Look, I am late for breakfast.' He gave Belle a quick pat on the head. 'My parents are waiting! See you around.'

Then he set off quickly up the hill, leaving Coco to wonder why everything was always so awkward, but more importantly:

A GHOST? Many years ago, at the hotel . . . ?

Something had happened there. But what on earth had he been meaning to say?

'You did it, well done!' said Dad as Coco plonked the baguette on to the long, messy kitchen table. The kitchen was old-fashioned, with pale yellow cupboards and ugly cream tiles, but there was space enough to seat an army around that table.

Belle shot off to sniff a dusty corner, her tail wagging at nothing.

'Cheryl, *ma chérie*,' said Dad, pouring water into the coffee machine as Mum set up her phone to film some sort of old jug thing on the far end of the table. 'Coco got the bread!' He still had bits of plaster in his beard.

'That's brilliant, sweetheart,' said Mum, looking up, her face still speckled with dust too. 'The more you practise French, the better you'll get.' She smiled, but it barely hid that *I'm worried about money* expression she wore a lot lately.

Her parents were always worried about money. Especially paying back that bank loan by Easter. Mum forced another smile. 'Oh, by the way, I saw a boy go into a house on the other side of the square. Did you see him?'

BANG!!!

The kitchen door suddenly slammed shut, making them all jump.

Belle barked.

An icy breeze blew past the table. Coco shuddered. The kitchen suddenly felt odd and chilly, like in her room at night and on that cold spot on the stairs.

Dad strode over to the door to open it again.

'Yeah, I saw him,' said Coco, but goose bumps were prickling up her neck. She tried to ignore them. 'He was in the bakery when I arrived.'

'Well?' said Mum. 'Did you talk to him? He looked about your age.'

Belle was howling now.

'Shush, Belle . . . No, I didn't,' Coco lied. She was still embarrassed for making such a fool of herself.

'Oh, shame,' said Mum, oblivious. 'Well, he lives on our square, so you should go and introduce yourself.' She paused. 'We all should, actually. Well, to his parents. And the lady who lives in that blue-shuttered house next door to them. It's just we've had so much to do here, haven't we? We haven't had time to meet anyone, yet.'

BANG! The kitchen door slammed again.

'AH!' Coco cried out this time. What on earth was going on?

Belle whined, but her tail was wagging.

'There must be a draught,' said Dad, getting up to open it again. 'Ha! That really made you jump, didn't it, Coco!'

Coco forced a smile, but her heart was racing. She thought back to what that boy Louis had said . . . about a gh—

No! she told herself. *Ghosts don't exist . . . Ghosts do NOT exist. Especially not in daylight.*

'Here, use this to stop the door,' said Mum, handing Dad the strange jug.

'What is it?' Coco asked, trying to sound normal.

'I'm guessing it's a coffee pot,' said Mum. 'It's quite heavy. We found it in here, at the back of an old cupboard. It's got the initials "H" and "F", which must stand for Hôtel Framboise. I'm going to film it for a post after breakfast.'

A chocolate smell wafted into Coco's nose and made her stomach tighten. It was just like the scent in her room.

'Can you smell that?' asked Dad.

'Ooh yes, it's like dark chocolate!' said Mum.

Belle could smell it too. She was sniffing the air.

'Maybe the pot was for chocolate. Not coffee,' Dad suggested, opening the lid. 'I bet there's some left in the bottom.'

But when Coco peered inside, it was empty.

CRASH!

It sounded like something had fallen on to the floor in the lobby.

Mum and Dad jumped up. Coco rushed out after them.

'Oh no!' Mum cried.

'Not the mirror!' whimpered Dad.

The huge, expensive antique mirror they'd bought for the lobby wall lay smashed on the old tile floor.

'Belle, stay away!'

'Isn't that seven years' bad luck?' said Coco, holding Belle's collar. She felt scared.

'Seven months' salary, more like!' said Mum. She looked ready to cry. 'After the hotel, that was the most expensive thing we've ever bought! Burt! I told you not to lean it on the tile boxes!'

Dad opened his mouth to argue, then sighed. 'I'll clean it up after breakfast.'

So they traipsed back to the kitchen table and Dad poured the coffee in worried silence, but Coco couldn't stop feeling uneasy. She felt like they were being watched and it made her all squirmy inside . . .

'Where's the bread?' She scanned the table, where she'd left the baguette. It was nowhere to be seen.

Then Mum spotted a corner of the baguette wrapping poking out from under the table.

Belle was sniffing at it.

'Oh, Belle!' Mum said, picking up the paper. 'You shouldn't eat bread – it gives you the runs!'

'Belle!' said Dad, with a sigh. 'That was naughty!'

7

'Oh, oh, oh!'

This was brilliant. *No.* Better than brilliant! This was *brillantissime*!

The ghost chuckled as he whooshed himself through the cupboard and back down into his secret workshop.

'Their faces!' He did a little jig. 'And the mirror. Ha!' He'd not planned that part, but it had worked a treat! 'Serves them right for using my chocolate pot as a door stop! She thought it'd bring them bad luck. Ha! I'll bring them bad luck all right. And they blamed the dog for the bread.' He laughed, and made a mental note to remember that the dog – 'Cute, intelligent, nicest one by far' – could see him and even understand him. She'd come to him *and* howled on command. Even better, he'd discovered that *he* could understand *her*. She'd wanted to roll over for a tummy tickle. He'd told her not to. Ha! Being dead did seem to come with some new perks. Maybe he could use them to his advantage at some point.

And then he laughed so hard he forgot to tell his body to stop moving through solid things, and he slipped through his old marble worktable straight into a sack of crystallized sugar. 'ZUT!'

He gathered himself together and shot back up to admire the baguette on the middle shelf. Shame he couldn't eat it. It smelt rather good. But never mind. It was his trophy now – like those horrible chocolate balls!

'I'll go back and take the pot later, too,' he told himself. What was it they thought it had been used for? 'Coffee! Pffft!' He shook his head disapprovingly. 'I'm glad they found it, though,' he admitted out loud. He'd thought it had vanished with the rest of his possessions, when those horrible officials had barged into the hotel just days after his death and emptied it of all his belongings.

He shuddered at the memory.

He'd only had time to salvage one thing: his beloved recipe book – which, thank goodness, he had already hidden. And they'd not found his workshop. *Dieu merci!*

He took the book out of his pocket and placed it on the shelf by his culinary loot, bent over to position his face just above the top of it, then . . .

WHOOSH!

. . . he shoved his head straight into it as if it were a bowl of water.

It was the fastest way to read. The words leapt off the page and into his head without the bother of page-turning. Spooks didn't have to abide by the physical rules of the living. It was, perhaps, the only perk of being dead.

'Mmmmm!' He licked his lips once he'd found the recipe for his favourite chocolate and vanilla cream.

'Oooh!' He sighed as he read about getting the chocolate to the right temperature.

'Ahhh!' He swooned with delight at the thought of piping velveteen fillings into delicate little shells of dark chocolate.

And then he stopped.

Because at the bottom of the page he'd made a note about using all five senses – touch, taste, sight, smell and hearing – to create the best sweet treats possible. And it had just given him a *hauntingly* good idea.

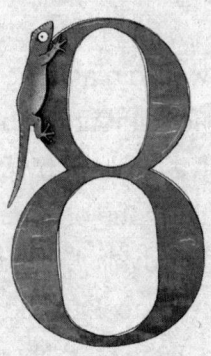

Now, if you'd just moved into a spooky hotel, where you'd seen and heard weird things, and you'd met a boy from the village who'd said there was a ghost, even though you'd been telling yourself that ghosts don't exist, then you'd probably be feeling like Coco: CONFUSED and a little bit SCARED!

The rest of the morning had passed without mishap: after a makeshift breakfast of grapes, she'd kept Mum company as she replastered Guest Room 1 (filming her every move), and Dad had both cleaned up the broken mirror and called the Wi-Fi people, who promised they'd come soon. So Coco should have felt happy.

BUT...

She didn't.

She couldn't shake the feeling that she was being

watched. Which was creepy.

The events in the kitchen and lobby had given her the same feeling of fear and unease as all the weird stuff in her bedroom.

What if all that door banging and mirror smashing and baguette disappearing wasn't just draughts, rickety tile piles and Belle being greedy, like Mum and Dad said? What if there really is a gh—?

Nope. She wouldn't finish that thought.

But things got even more confusing when she took Belle out for a walk by the old tower before lunch and her dog did a perfectly formed doo-doo. Coco wouldn't normally have paid much attention to the size and shape of the poo, but this time she did, because it meant Belle didn't have 'the runs', which meant she couldn't have eaten the bread, which meant that something else had happened to the baguette. Which meant . . .

What did it mean? Baguettes didn't just disappear.

And the worst thing was, Coco couldn't talk to Mum and Dad about her worries. They were too busy with the hotel. But also because whenever they'd seen a 'doer-upper' (Mum and Dad's term for a French renovation project) on TV and Coco had commented on its spooky appearance, they'd replied, 'Nah! It's just run-down. All old places look like that until you pour love and hard work into them.' If she said she was scared, they'd say she was being silly, or that she was playing up because she didn't want to live in France.

Anyway. Maybe I am being silly? Coco thought. *I definitely don't want to live in France! And I definitely, absolutely don't believe in ghosts.*

Still, that 'being watched' feeling wouldn't go away, so that afternoon, she tried to ignore it by heading outside to read. And for a while – book in hand in the balmy sunshine, with Belle snoring at her feet, and tiny wall lizards rustling through the raspberry bushes into their hidey-holes – she felt OK.

But as the sun began to set and a chilly breeze began to blow, Coco felt as though someone had thrown a thick veil over the entire hotel and something dark and mischievous was brewing inside.

It made her shiver.

And feel a little bit sick.

And not want to go to sleep alone.

'Can I take Belle to bed with me tonight?' she asked after dinner as they played Monopoly in the kitchen (there was still no sitting room or TV). It was a Burton-on-the-Bush version of the game, and it made her heart ache as she saw all the familiar street names.

'No, sorry, Coco.' Mum put a hotel on Bush Lane, then stood up to close the window. Coco sighed. Bush Lane was where Choco-Yum-Yums was.

'We don't want Belle getting used to going upstairs to the bedrooms. It might put the guests off. Not everyone loves dogs like us.'

And so, it was with a heavy heart that Coco eventually said, 'Night', kissed Belle, who whined as if saying, 'Sorry I can't come', then dragged herself up three rickety flights of stairs to bed, alone, her palms clammy and her stomach tight. She had a sinking feeling that the night was going to be long.

But . . .

She was WRONG!

That's right.

NOTHING happened.

Not even the sighing and the footsteps.

And when she finally woke up the next morning, she was surprised to discover that she'd slept quite well.

She rushed downstairs for breakfast and found that the ground floor felt different too.

It felt lighter.

Less . . . unfriendly. Which was confusing.

Not a day before, she'd felt nothing but dread all over the property. But now, moving through the hotel, from the lobby, into the five shabby bedrooms on the first floor, then up the stairs to Mum and Dad's room, and into the other five guest rooms, she felt nothing but . . . dust and cobwebs, which tickled her face and made her sneeze.

And to her delight, this peaceful atmosphere filled the hotel for the next few days, too.

I must have imagined it all, she told herself. How silly she'd been.

That week, Coco managed to:

- Wave to Louis across the square.
- Film Mum putting up flowery wallpaper in the first guest room.
- Follow the Wi-Fi people around the hotel. She didn't understand a word, but Dad told her they'd have a connection soon.
- Drive with Mum, past purple fields of lustrous lavender and brown-green olive groves, to the nearest big town, so Mum could start uploading the videos to her profile and do a big shop in a *hypermarché* (one of those huge French supermarkets that sold almost everything).
- Send and receive a few messages in the 'Best Friends – England to France' chat she had with Kate and Rose while they were at the shop.

They read:

ROSE
Mum's dyed her hair pink for charity!

KATE
I got a new rabbit! She's called Chelsea Bun-Bun.

ROSE

Summer holidays start tomorrow for us!

KATE

Next Choco-Yum-Yums class is mint choc chip cupcakes! Wish you were doing it with us!

ROSE

Here's the recipe. We miss you!

COCO

Me too ☹

Coco smiled. Her friends missed her! And had sent the recipe. Which was nice. It made her feel a little less lonely. But – she sighed – it also reminded her how far away they were now.

By the end of the week, Coco had decided that the spooky stuff must really all have been in her head. Yes, Belle had been looking up at the lobby ceiling, wagging her tail at nothing again, but that didn't mean anything, because the dread she'd felt had simply gone. What a relief!

But then came the STORM.

It was the thunder that first woke Coco. A grumbling, angry roar, followed by battering rain and howling winds. It made the shutters on the windows rattle and the walls creak.

But that wasn't what scared her.

What scared her was . . .

KNOCK! THUD!

Coco immediately sat up – her heart racing. What had made *that* noise? It sounded like it had come from inside the hotel, not outside in the storm. She pulled her duvet up around her neck. Were her parents still up doing work? Her eyes darted through the semi-darkness to her clock: 12.03 a.m. No. Mum and Dad would be asleep by now, which meant . . .

It had to be something else.

Please don't let it be starting again! she thought, as

memories of the previous horrors flooded back in icy waves.

But (as I'm sure you can guess), it was starting again. Big time.

KNOCK! THUD! KNOCK!

She gulped, then sank further into her covers. The noises had come from inside her wardrobe. Which was RIGHT NEXT TO HER BED.

'It's not real. It's not real,' she whispered.

But it was real all right. As real as . . .

'HE-HOR-HE-HOOOOOOR!'

'HE-HOR-HE-HOOOOOOR!'

. . . the echoey moan that suddenly filled the room. And . . .

WHOOSH!

. . . the howling wind that suddenly burst in through the window.

The gust was so strong it made the curtains billow.

And suddenly the hammering rain outside was blowing inside in diagonal sheets.

It was a warm summer storm, but weird icy air puffed on her cheeks.

BAM!

Coco shook in terror as her wardrobe door swung open like a sideways jack-in-the-box.

She wanted to scream, but no sound would come out.

All she could do was stare as . . .

CREAK!

. . . A foot. A black, shadowy foot, connected to – she thought she'd faint – a figure that drifted out and took shape at the foot of her bed.

Legs . . .

Body . . .

Arms . . .

A frightening frame assembling itself like a ghastly doll. And as it went, its thick black substance (whatever that was) was turning eerily translucent as the smell of chocolate filled the air.

FLASH!

Lightning lit it up from behind.

It was a man!

He looked like a ghoulish, life-size shadow puppet.

Coco had had enough.

Her survival switch flicked on inside her head – she wasn't waiting to see the rest.

She grabbed her phone and shot out of her room like a bullet, speeding down three flights of stairs to the kitchen.

OK, now I believe in ghosts! Now *I believe in ghosts!* her brain screamed, as she switched on the light and crawled into Belle's basket, where she lay trembling, hugging the still-sleeping dog for comfort.

Coco didn't want to think it. She really didn't. But what she had just seen upstairs had been as real as the goose bumps prickling over her arms and the shivers still coursing down her spine.

She felt shocked. And frightened. And worried. Then – as she felt Belle breathing (blissfully unaware of Coco's state and the horrors she'd just witnessed in the attic) and her eyes fell on her parents' tools laid out messily on the kitchen table – she felt something else too: ANGER.

She'd had enough.

OF EVERYTHING.

Her crumbling home.

Living in France.

Having to change schools.

Missing her friends.

Not speaking French.

The non-existent Wi-Fi.

But she'd especially had enough of THE GHOST!

How dare WHATEVER or WHOEVER this thing was try to spook her and her family! There one minute, disappearing the next. It was as if he was playing with her.

And in that moment, she knew.

Like it or lump it, she was going to get rid of him.

She didn't know how yet, but she'd work it out.

For herself. For Mum. For Dad. For Belle.

10

'Ha! Ha! Ha! I'm a ghoulish genius!' the ghost cried (in French, of course). 'A phantasmal prodigy! An entity extraordinaire!'

He floated up to the ceiling with joy. That storm! It had been exactly what he'd needed. Who'd have thought he had such naughtiness in him? When he'd been alive, he'd been a pillar of respectability. But now? Well . . . this was fun! He'd wanted to be theatrical, but even he couldn't have timed the lightning better. Ooooh! It had worked a treat.

'If that wasn't the stuff nightmares are made of, I don't know what is!' he said, patting the recipe book in his pocket.

Using the five senses in a haunting had worked so well! The storm had set the tone, but he'd done:

- The Knocking and the HE-HOR-HE-HORing for Hearing
- His translucent apparition for Sight
- His usual chocolate scent for Smell
- Icy puffs blown on her cheeks for Touch

The only sense he hadn't done was Taste, but he'd work on that for another time – to really crank up the fear. Maybe he could turn something in the kitchen into something rotten? *Oh joy!*

And clinging to that marvellous thought, he looked out through the open window, over the village square, at the house with the blue shutters.

11

Coco had been too scared and angry to sleep, but exhaustion got her in the end.

She woke with a start at 8 a.m., Belle licking her ear, thinking for one wonderful moment that she was back in her old bed in England – until she saw the kitchen. Then the horrors of the previous night – the storm, the sounds, the wind, the ghost – flooded over her like a tidal wave and she wanted to cry.

But no.

'I'm on a mission!' she told herself, tapping her foot on the floor. It had gone to sleep in the cramped dog basket and was all pins and needles. 'A ghost-busting mission!'

It felt funny saying that out loud. In one day, she'd gone from not wanting to believe in ghosts to half believing to utterly believing.

But who wouldn't after what she'd seen? She'd never been more terrified in her life.

Mum and Dad were still in bed, so she tiptoed to the laundry room to find something to wear from the ironing basket, because . . . well, she didn't fancy going back to her room yet (and can you blame her?). And then, sensing that the ghost wasn't around (there was no heavy atmosphere, and she didn't feel watched), she got dressed, gave Belle her breakfast, then sat down at the kitchen table to think.

If she was going to get rid of the ghost, she needed to know as much about him as possible.

And what she knew so far was . . . *Hmmm!* What did she know?

That he was a ghost.

Of a man.

Who was dead (obviously, or he wouldn't be a ghost).

Who smelt of chocolate – which was weird.

And then her embarrassing encounter with Louis popped back into her head.

He'd asked if she'd seen a ghost and said that something had happened at the hotel.

Well, she was going to find out what. She leapt to her feet. Louis had lived in this village longer than she had. Embarrassment or no embarrassment, she was going to have to talk to him . . .

'Oh! You're up?' Mum burst into the kitchen with a packet of cornflakes in one hand.

'Yeah,' said Coco, quickly sitting back down, trying not to let on that her entire world had just changed.

'Want a bowl?'

'Yes, please,' she answered, though she wasn't hungry.

'I found them in a box I was unpacking upstairs. Did you hear the storm last night?' She turned to Coco. 'Oh! You look pale, sweetheart. Are you feeling OK?'

'Yes!' Coco squeaked. But she wanted to shout, *NO, I AM NOT OK. WOULD YOU BE OK IF YOU'D JUST BEEN SPOOKED BY A GHOST? A REAL-LIFE, WARDROBE-KNOCKING, HOWLING, FRENCH GHOUL!* But she didn't. She knew Mum would never believe her.

'I'm fine.' Coco gave Mum a reassuring kiss on the cheek. 'I just didn't sleep well in the storm, that's all!'

'Well, I'm not surprised,' said Mum, filling the bowls and pouring the milk. 'With all that banging and moaning and creaking, anyone would have thought we had a ghost in the rafters! Ha!'

Coco marched across the square without letting Belle stop for so much as a sniff. And she was so determined to ask Louis what he knew that she forgot she might have to speak French – until she arrived in front of the row of houses and realized she didn't remember which one was

Louis's. Then the usual panic set in: pounding heart, sweaty palms, wobbly legs . . .

There were three houses in a row. The left one looked abandoned. It had ivy growing over the cracked windows and a rusty metal shutter covering the door. The middle one had blue shutters, and the right one had a window box full of pink and purple flowers.

I'll try the middle one, she thought. And then, taking her courage into both (shaky) hands, she knocked.

'Please let it be Louis, please let it be Louis,' she whispered, preparing herself to pronounce the French word for 'Hello', which she knew perfectly well was '*Bonjour*'.

But it wasn't Louis.

It was a white-haired older lady with piercing grey eyes and a walking stick. Coco had never seen her before.

And the shock of it made her mouth dry and her tongue twist and her lips move in a way she didn't intend, and instead of *Bonjour* she said, '*Bon jus!*', which – she realized as it came out – meant 'nice fruit juice'.

Coco cringed.

The woman frowned, then eyed Coco and Belle from head to toe to tail.

'Erm . . .' Coco panicked. 'I'm so sorry, *madame*.' (She knew it was polite to address French grown-ups as *madame* for a lady and *monsieur* for a man, so hoped it would make up for the mistake.) 'I'm Coco. I live in the hotel. I meant to . . . erm . . . say—'

'I know where you live,' said the woman in accented English.

'Oh . . . right! Good,' said Coco, squirming. 'I'm looking for Louis. Does he live here?'

'Louis?' said the woman. She pointed at the next house and then slammed the door.

Well, that went well! thought Coco. In two seconds flat she'd made a fool out of herself. Again. And had a door slammed in her face.

Her eye caught the name of the lady's letterbox. It read 'Madame M. Auguste'. 'I wish I'd seen that before,' she said to herself. 'I wouldn't have knocked.'

Oh why, oh why had her family had to move to France? Ghosts, the embarrassment of speaking French . . . She'd never have had to deal with any of this if they'd stayed in Burton-on-the-Bush.

But she had a haunting to stop.

So, holding that thought, she knocked on next door's door.

And to her relief a boy with dark eyes and black glasses opened it.

Coco was so pleased, she didn't even say 'hello'.

She just stood at the doorstep and announced: 'Louis, I've seen him. I've seen the ghost!'

'You have seen him?' Louis whispered, his eyes wide.

'Yes!' said Coco. 'You *have* to tell me everything you know.'

'Ooh, everything you know about what?' A lady with a dark brown bob and a broad smile appeared behind Louis.

'Oh, just things about . . . the village, Maman,' Louis said, giving Coco a look that meant *don't say anything else about the G. H. O. S. T.* Coco supposed it was because his parents didn't believe in that sort of thing either.

'*Bonjour!* You must be Coco!' said Louis's mum, shaking Coco's hand, before crouching down to pet Belle. 'You're a pretty dog!' she cooed. And like her son, her English was excellent – better even. Belle licked her cheek and said, 'Woo-woo-woo!' 'Louis said he'd met you. How are you settling in?'

'Very well, thank you,' Coco lied.

'Good! Well, you must tell your parents we'll introduce ourselves very soon. Oh, and give them this.' From a little wooden cupboard in the flowery hallway, she got out a jar and a paper bag. 'It's our homemade lavender jam!'

'Thank you!' said Coco. The bag had little drawings of lavender and butterflies on it, set around the word *Confiture*, which Coco knew meant 'jam'.

'It's so lovely to see people finally renovating the hotel,' Louis's mum continued. 'Louis, we're going out this afternoon, but if Coco wants to know about the village, why not take some time to show her around this morning?'

'*Bonne idée*,' he replied, giving Coco a wide-eyed stare that meant, *just go along with it*. 'Have you seen the Murder Cave yet?'

'Murder Cave? No.' What sort of place was that?

'It is very cool,' he replied, seeing the uncertain expression on her face. 'And a good place to talk without parents,' he whispered, bending down to put his shoes on, before speaking loudly again. 'It is from hundreds of years ago, when the castle was more than just the tower. It is at the top of the hill, and prisoners were left there to die, without food or water. All they could do was look out over the countryside and hope for an escape . . . that never came!'

'Sounds lovely,' Coco squeaked.

Louis and Coco set off in the sunshine with Belle (and the jam) – over a rickety stone wall, down a dusty slope and along a stony path hidden by bright yellow flowering gorse bushes – towards the edge of the village. On the way, Coco told Louis all about what had happened in her room. She hadn't meant to speak first. Or even tell him everything. But as they walked, she was so desperate to talk about it to someone who might believe her, that she forgot she didn't know him very well and spoke non-stop.

And Louis listened.

And didn't laugh or scoff once.

And when they climbed up some old stone steps into the Murder Cave and looked out over the countryside, he briefly took advantage of a pause in Coco's tale to tell her that the stripy fields of lavender below the white, lace-like rocks up ahead belonged to his family, and that there were holes in the cave wall where the prison bars would once have been.

Belle sniffed at one, and Coco noticed a small, rolled-up piece of old card stuffed into it, so she picked at it, without thinking, then – when it fell out – put it into her cardigan pocket.

Then, she told Louis all about how the ghost had burst

out of her wardrobe, and Louis stared at her with wide eyes that said, *Rather you than me!*

Then it was his turn:

'*Bah*, I cannot beat your story,' he said. He looked like it was both the worst and best thing he'd ever heard. 'All I know is what my mum told me. Years ago, the owner of the hotel, Monsieur Framboise, died there, and it must have been bad, because after he died, people started moving out of the village and the shops started closing.'

'What do you mean, *must have been bad*?' cried Coco. Things were getting worse by the minute. 'How did he die?'

Louis shrugged. 'It is a mystery. Mum was a little girl when it happened. Only four families are here now. *Cinq* . . . five, including yours. There is us, because the lavender farm has been in the family of my mother for years; Madame Tiffet, the baker, but her children are grown-up now and live in Paris; and Monsieur Dubois, at Café de la Poste. He runs the post office too. I do not think he has ever had a family. Oh, and Madame Auguste.'

'I met her,' said Coco. 'I knocked on her door first by mistake. I don't think she likes me.'

'She likes no one,' said Louis. 'The only time she leaves her house or the village is on Wednesdays to go shopping. Nobody knows her story. She is scary.'

'Well, that dead owner – Monsieur Framboise – must

be the ghost,' said Coco.

'That is what I think too,' said Louis. 'That is why he looks out of the windows all the time!'

'WHAT?! Which windows?'

'All of them. Your kitchen, the hotel bedrooms, the attic. I have been seeing him since I was a little boy. Mum and Dad say it is just my imagination. But I know it is not. That is why I asked you.'

Coco gasped. In the photos she'd taken the other day, there'd been a blob in the kitchen window. She'd thought it was dirt, but . . . She scrolled through her phone, found the photos then zoomed in . . . and there, sure enough, was the face of a man. It was a bit blurry and grey – like an old black-and-white postcard – but there was no mistaking it. A round, sad face, with a moustache that curled upwards.

'Was this who you saw?' she said, holding the phone out to Louis with a wobbly hand.

'Yes!' Louis looked up like he'd seen a ghost (which, of course, he just had, again). 'When did you take it?'

'The day we met at the bakery.'

The new friends – for yes, that is what they had just become (sharing a haunting can do that to you) – just sat there in silence for a moment, taking it all in.

Then Coco said thoughtfully, 'Louis, we've got to get rid of this Monsieur Framboise ghost person. I don't think I can live here if he keeps haunting us. But how do you bust ghosts? I read a book once, where a man threw salt at one.'

'What happened?'

'It frazzled and disappeared.'

'*Bien*,' said Louis. 'I read one time that ghosts hang around when they have something left they have not done.'

'You mean unfinished business?'

'*Oui*. Maybe that is what you must do? Find out what his unfinished business is or was so he can leave?'

'But do you think either will work?'

Louis shrugged. 'But the next village, Bellevue, has got a library, with Wi-Fi on the computers. I am not allowed internet on my phone.'

'Me neither,' said Coco.

'We can see if there is anything online about his death.'

'Or about ways to get rid of ghosts,' Coco added, thinking of the salt.

'Yes. And it is open this morning. If we go very fast, we will get there before it closes. Have you got a bike?'

13

Mum and Dad were over the moon when Coco gave them the jam and asked if she could cycle with Louis to the library. Dad found her bike behind some old picture frames and immediately dusted it down. Belle went in to finish her breakfast.

'Just take your phone,' said Mum.

'And be careful,' said Dad.

'We will,' said Coco, kissing Belle goodbye.

And once Louis (who peered nervously in from the front step) had reassured them that he did the trip over the fields all the time and that they wouldn't be going on any main roads, Coco saw her parents give each other a *now-she's-made-a-friend-everything-will-be-all-right* look. But she knew it wouldn't.

Not until she stopped missing Kate and Rose . . .

And Burton-on-the-Bush . . .

And her baking classes . . .

And ESPECIALLY NOT until they'd managed to get rid of the GHOST!

She suddenly felt nervous about leaving her parents and Belle alone in the hotel. *But nothing's happened to them so far*, she reassured herself. *And if I say anything, Mum and Dad won't believe me. I just need to fix the problem. Fast.*

So, she waved goodbye, then followed Louis over the square to whizz down Mont-Lavande's bumpy, cobbled hill, past the bakery and Café de la Poste – where Madame Tiffet was sipping coffee on the terrace with Monsieur Dubois, alongside a few resting hikers. The morning wind was already so warm, it was like riding through a very bouncy hairdryer.

At the bottom of the hill, they turned off on to a dusty path that led past Louis's family's farm and straight into the lavender fields. And that was like riding through a sachet of Dad's herbal tea, with long, thick rows of lavender, spiked with rosemary, thyme and, at the end of each line, rose bushes.

The path was bumpy here too. Coco had to swerve to avoid clumps of hard mud and dodge the occasional bee, which, she thought, must live in the hives she could see at the edge of the field, by a copse of gnarly olive trees.

She couldn't imagine anywhere on Earth more different from Burton-on-the-Bush. She still didn't want to be here, but maybe not all of it was bad.

For every shop and red-brick house back home, here was something bursting out of the ground with flowers. And for every noisy car, bus or bin truck outside her old house, here were cicadas (little winged insects), chirruping loudly among the undergrowth.

They turned on to a track that led into a little patch of woodland, and Louis got off his bike before pulling his notebook and pencil from his pocket.

'What are you doing?' Coco asked, getting off her bike too. Louis was crouching over a tall plant with dark purple, bell-shaped flowers.

He glanced up, suddenly looking a bit shy. 'Drawing. This plant does not flower until now, so I have been waiting for it.'

Coco leant over his shoulder. His notebook was full of little sketches of plants and flowers.

'Wow! These are amazing, Louis!'

He blushed. 'I could take photos on my phone, but I prefer to draw them.'

'Well, you're really good at it! Seriously!'

Coco bent over to touch the flowers.

'STOP!' Louis shouted.

'Why?'

'It is deadly nightshade! Everything about it can kill you – even touching it!'

'What?' Coco whipped her hand back.

'The flowers look pretty now, then soon the berries will look like delicious blueberries. But touch one – worse, eat one – and it will be *au revoir*!'

'How do you know all this?' Coco asked, stunned.

'When you grow up on a lavender farm, you have to learn lots about flowers and nature.'

That made sense. But Coco was still impressed. She tried him out: 'What's that?' she said, pointing.

'A cypress tree.'

'And this?'

'A pine.'

'And this mushroom?' Coco pointed with her shoe.

'Erm, that is a stone!'

'I knew that!' said Coco.

They giggled and got back on their bikes. Then they left behind the green wood and purple deadly nightshade for another colour: yellow! Endless fields of smiley yellow sunflowers – all at least double the height of their bikes.

Then it was a twist around a big white rock here, and a turn past an old farmhouse there, and they found themselves on a steep slope, puffing up towards the hilltop village of Bellevue – more lived-in than

Mont-Lavande, with narrower winding streets and redder stone buildings that stood out against the bright blue sky. And it was in front of one of them, where a sign read '*Bibliothèque*', that they stopped and parked their bikes.

Coco had expected the inside of the library to be as old as the outside, but when they stepped in, the air was cool, and everywhere was white and modern, with bookshelves in neat labelled sections.

Louis asked if they could use the library internet, so the librarian led them to a computer at the back – 'With child settings!' he said with a wink.

Coco typed 'Hôtel Framboise Mont-Lavande' into a search and thought she'd die.

There was Mum's account! The top search result. Her dust-speckled face grinning back at them from alongside paint rollers and brushes and sacks of cement and tools and boxes of tiles and the chocolate pot and the –ATIER letters of the fallen facade. And she only had a few likes. This was so embarrassing!

'Erm, let's see what else there is,' Coco said, clicking back quickly.

'Well, this is our farm website. Ferme Martin,' Louis said matter-of-factly, clicking on the second result and clearly not thinking there was anything wrong with

Coco's mum's hotel feed. He showed her all the photos of lavender fields and jams and essential oils and perfume and honey and other fragrant things his family sold, then he clicked on the only other result. 'An old news article about the hotel.'

'What does it say?'

'That someone called Isidore Framboise died in it on Valentine's Day, 1981.'

'Isidore?' said Coco. The name felt funny on her tongue. 'Isidore Framboise! So that's our ghost's full name. Now let's see how we can get rid of him.'

'What must I type in English for that?' Louis asked.

'*Ways to bust a ghost*, maybe?' said Coco. 'With a "h" in ghost,' she added, correcting Louis's spelling as he typed (and secretly happy to have taught him something in English).

A few things popped up:

Placing iron chains in doorways . . .

Ringing silver bells . . .

But nothing they could do.

'Where do you even buy chains and bells?' Coco frowned. 'You keep looking. I'll try the books.'

Louis pointed to the *Fantastique* (scary story) section, so Coco set off, scanning the shelves for the word '*fantôme*', which she knew from school meant 'ghost'. But all she found was *Le Fantôme de Canterville* by Oscar

Wilde, which she supposed was *The Canterville Ghost*, and *Le Fantôme de l'Opéra* by Gaston Leroux, which she knew was *The Phantom of the Opera*.

She tried other shelves.

There was one marked *Sciences*, another *Littérature* and another *Voyages*, then her eyes wondered to a section marked *Histoire Locale*. She knew *histoire* meant 'history', and *locale* looked like 'local'. *I wonder if there's anything here about the hotel*, she thought. If she could find something about its history, it might help her find out the ghost's unfinished business.

Her eyes scanned the shelves from left to right. Some books were shabby, others brand new; most just looked really old. Then suddenly, one title caught her eye: *L'Histoire de Mont-Lavande*.

The History of Mont-Lavande! Her heart did a little jump.

'I have not found anything useful,' said Louis, joining her again.

'It might not matter, Louis, look.' She pulled the book off the shelf. 'Maybe there's something about the hotel in it . . .'

She opened the book at the contents page.

'There is a section on the Murder Cave,' said Louis. 'And a drawing of what the castle would have looked like in medieval times.'

It was a fearsome-looking fortress, with long battlements.

'There's the tower,' said Coco. 'But there's no church.'

Then Louis pointed to a line marked *Destruction*. 'Ooh, it says here that the castle was destroyed in the fourteenth century by the English! Thanks, Coco!' He gave her a teasing nudge.

'I wasn't even born then!' She nudged him back.

'Then it says the village was built on top of where it once stood, in the nineteenth century,' Louis continued.

'That makes sense,' said Coco. 'There's "1831" carved in the stone over the hotel door.'

Coco flicked through some more pages. In one photo you could see the village square filled with old-fashioned-looking people going about their business in shops and cafes. Several of them had stopped to look at the camera. In another, the abandoned building next to Madame Auguste's house looked like it had once been a perfume shop. And the people in front of it were playing *boules* under the trees.

Coco gasped. On the next page was a photo of a smartly dressed young man with a round head and an upwards-curling moustache, standing in front of the hotel. 'Monsieur Framboise! And look, the date below says *1980*.'

Coco and Louis just stared at it for a moment, in

silence. It felt odd looking at the full-bodied, living version of the ghostly man who was trying to terrify her. There was nothing scary about him in the picture. He looked quite happy.

She said this to Louis, and he replied, 'Well, probably did not know he only had a year left to live. He looks younger than my parents in this photo.'

Coco's eyes searched the image to see if she could make out what was written on the hotel facade behind him, but it was too blurry. Louis read the nearby text, but all it said was that there had once been a hotel on the square – nothing more about its owner.

'Well, that was a waste of time,' Coco complained as they rode back on their bikes, past the sunflowers and a grey-haired man taking photos of the fields from his flashy open-top red sports car.

'No, it was not!' said Louis. 'We saw a photo of the ghost. We know that he died on *Saint-Valentin* in 1981. And that he was called Isidore.'

'S'pose,' said Coco, but she had a ball in her stomach. She was no closer to knowing how to fight him. And things got worse when she skidded up to the front of the hotel and Louis reminded her he had to go out that afternoon.

'Text me, OK?' he said.

'Yes,' she whispered, thinking, *If the sketchy network lets me.*

Coco stepped into the lobby, suddenly feeling scared. When she'd been with Louis, her ghost-busting task had felt doable – like a team project. Now, she was all alone . . .

That *scaredy* feeling stayed with Coco for the rest of the day – even when the Wi-Fi people came to set everything up and she *could* text Louis from upstairs, and finally use Mum's computer to video-call Kate and Rose from the kitchen (the old hotel walls were too thick for a strong signal to reach her room). Her friends were both at Kate's house watching their favourite baking programme, *Bake the Day*. Then they were going bowling.

It made Coco's life feel more unreal – as if she were living in a dream. *A nightmare, more like*, she thought. *My friends are going bowling. I'm going to fight a ghost!*

They weren't just living in different countries; they were living in different worlds.

And it didn't help that Coco caught Belle in their future guest breakfast room at the back of the lobby, wagging her tail at nothing again. Coco ushered Belle into the kitchen, then went straight for the cupboard to find the salt, shoving some in her pocket as a weapon. *It's better than nothing*, she thought. She dashed upstairs to plant the rest under her bed, her heart racing with fear.

By dinner time, all Coco could think about was the ghost, and how to use the salt against it. She didn't have a clue. Then, after dinner, as she and Mum and Dad played *jeu de l'oie* ('game of the goose', a sort of French version of snakes and ladders) in the kitchen, she found herself blurting out, 'Louis said the old owner died in the hotel.'

To which Mum answered, 'Ooh, did he? We've read so little history about the place. I'd love to know more.'

Then Dad, who'd noticed Coco's worried expression, replied, 'Don't worry about it, Coco. People die in buildings all the time. It doesn't mean anything. It's just part of life. It's our place, now.'

Yeah? Well tell that to the ghost! thought Coco. She had no proof Monsieur Framboise would be back that night, but the air felt thick, like the last time he had appeared.

And then, before she knew it, it was time for bed. For everyone . . .

'I'm pooped!' said Mum.

'Bedfordshire for me too!' Dad announced.

'I'll put Belle in her basket, then go up,' said Coco, looking for ways to stall. She did not want to go to her room. She texted Louis:

The ghost is watching me, I can feel it.

His reply came quickly:

You can do this! Don't let him win.

But Coco felt sick with fear.

She snuggled up to Belle's soft fur for so long that the clock turned midnight. Mum and Dad were bound to be snoring by now. She wanted to stay with her dog all night. But she had no choice. If she was going to get rid of this . . . this Monsieur-Framboise-person-thing – for her family, for her – she HAD to climb those stairs.

GULP!

The more she climbed, the more the air felt heavy – almost gloopy, like walking through invisible syrup.

She got to the top of the stairs, opened her door and slowly, carefully dared to feel for the light switch with her hand.

Peering in, she saw everything was just as she'd left it. Trembling, she dashed to her bed and grabbed the salt box from underneath it.

Now all she had to do was wait.

*

It didn't take long.

KNOCK! THUD! KNOCK!

It was coming from her wardrobe again. That familiar ball of fear filled her tummy. *Ignore it, ignore it*, she ordered herself. This was her moment. Her first (and hopefully last) ghost-busting mission. She mustn't be scared.

But . . . but . . . what should she do?

If the ghost was in her wardrobe, she couldn't get it with the salt without opening the doors, and she didn't want to leave her bed.

Maybe I should protect myself with salt, instead? she thought, and immediately chucked some in the air over her head. But all it did was fall everywhere like a bad case of dandruff! Head, shoulders . . . it was worse than a shampoo ad. She even had to blink salt out of her eyelashes.

She must have looked funny, but the situation was too dire to laugh, because . . .

DONK!

Her paper lightshade was swinging again.

Then . . .

POP! The bulb fizzed and died.

BANG!! The wardrobe door suddenly flew open.

Coco wanted to scream.

Nibby's chocolate balls were rolling out of the

wardrobe on to the wooden floor like spooky marbles, their red shiny paper glinting in the moonlight. And it made her feel sick, for those were the missing chocolates from downstairs and she knew they'd not been in her room before.

WORSE!

They should have rolled to a standstill, but instead, they whooshed off – one by one – across her floorboards towards the moonlit window where . . . a SHADOW was FORMING! Just like before, but blacker and denser, like a thick mist pouring itself into a floating, invisible mould, shaped like . . . was that a TALL HAT? It was hovering a foot off the floor!

Coco couldn't breathe. She frantically poured more salt into her hands.

'TAKE THAT!' she shouted, throwing it at the shape.

Sparks fizzed as the salt hit, causing the thing to whizz around the room like a firework – a gurgling firework. 'GGGA-GGGA!'

Had she done it? *Maybe!* thought Coco, amazed . . . The ghost in the film had frazzled before it had disappeared.

But the gurgle quickly turned into . . . a GIGGLE! And not just any giggle – a strong, echoey, gosh-that-tickles sort of giggle. Then the body came back into view – a fully formed Monsieur Framboise-shaped shadow now that whooshed through the air.

Coco threw more salt at him as he flew past, just in case she'd misunderstood the sound.

'HA HA HA!'

Nope. The laughter and sparkles got louder and brighter.

It wasn't working! The realization made her muscles stiffen and her throat tighten, and before she knew it, fear was filling her tummy again and making her want to cry.

'NO!' she cried out loud, as a strong, cold gust whipped around her room. *I won't let him win. He's dead. I'm alive. I'll show him I'm not scared!* And without thinking, she leapt out of bed and made a dash for the Nibby's chocolate balls, grabbing three.

Then she stood there, his icy wind whipping her cheeks. 'Hey you! You stole them!' she cried. 'So you eat them.' She threw the chocolates at the ghost, who watched in surprise as they passed straight through him and hit the skirting board.

And that's when it happened.

'What in the name of chocolate cream are you doing?'

The voice was distant and echoey – like someone bellowing from the end of a long tunnel.

Then, as the wind died down, there was Monsieur Framboise – more than just a shadow.

She could see his arms, outstretched towards her, and his face – the same round, moustachioed head as in the photo – with cold eyes, glowing like blue ice.

Coco wanted to scream, but her mouth just gaped open like a goldfish.

His silhouette was filling out to reveal . . . a white jacket, white trousers, black boots and . . . what *was* that on his head? A tall white hat? Like the shape he'd made just before. *Like a chef.*

And something else was emanating from him too, which Coco understood all too well: loneliness. Deep-rooted loneliness. The sort that comes after decades of being alone.

Then he shook his head at Coco, and holding her gaze, clicked his fingers.

The Nibby's she'd just thrown at him immediately flew up from the floor and into his outstretched hand, which he brought up to his nose to sniff. Then he cried, 'How dare you insult me! *Moi?* Eat these . . . these . . . abominations? They're only twenty per cent *cacao*!'

Coco thought she'd faint. The way he'd said it was like wind howling down a chimney. It made the hairs on her neck prickle.

'Y-you can tell how much cocoa there is just from the smell?' she said, despite herself, and though her voice was quite clear, her insides felt like mush.

'*Oui, oui* . . . Of course!' he snapped.

All sorts of thoughts arrived in Coco's mind at the

same time:

I'm talking to him.

He seems to know a lot about chocolate.

Louis, Louis, why aren't you seeing this?

ARGH! HELP ME, BELLE!

Coco looked at his clothes again and his tall white hat – quite unlike the suit he'd been wearing in the book photo. 'D-did you used to be a chef?' she dared to ask, not quite sure whether to run away or stay.

But there was no time for a reply.

Coco recognized the sound of Mum's footsteps on the stairs.

The ghost must have heard them too, for he suddenly roared, 'CHILD!'

'I have a name!' she yelled. 'Coco Bean!'

'Is that a joke?' bellowed the ghost.

'No,' said Coco. 'Like Chanel, not chocolate. And I know you're Isidore Framboise!'

The ghost looked shocked at the sound of his name – as though he'd not heard it pronounced for decades, which Coco thought must be the case.

'Well, Coco-Chanel-not-chocolate, you will meet me in the wine cellar at midnight tomorrow. I will show you what real *chocolat* is! Not this rubbish!' Then, with an echoey 'BE THEEEERE!', he pocketed the last two chocolates and disappeared into thin air.

'What are you doing?' said Mum, bursting into the room with Belle at her heels. Belle immediately jumped on to Coco and licked her cheek, as if feeling her distress. 'It's one in the morning. I heard voices.'

'I just . . . erm . . . I had a nightmare,' Coco lied, her head swirling. She was out of breath too. She couldn't believe what had just happened. 'I must have been talking in my sleep.'

Mum made to close the window, but just as she did, an enormous bang came from outside the hotel. Mum and Coco looked at each other for a moment.

'Quick!' Mum cried.

Coco followed her downstairs and out the front door.

Belle dashed out after them, barking, followed by Dad, rubbing his eyes.

There on the pavement was more plaster from the front of the hotel. And in the pale light of the square's only street lamp were not just the letters ATIER, but the full word:

CHOCOLATIER

15

Non! Non! Non! What have I just done? thought Monsieur Framboise as he whooshed back to his secret workshop. He'd never felt so confused!

One minute he'd been a perfect picture of horror, pouring himself into an invisible chef's-hat-shaped mould like phantasmagorical jelly – a fabulous mix of culinary skills and intimidation that he'd invented!

The next he'd been tickled by flying salt!

Oh, the humiliation!

But then, just as he'd been about to get his own back on her (he'd planned to shake the bottom of her bed with a terrifying 'woooooo!'), she'd thrown those low-quality Nibby's at him, then . . . well . . . he'd not been able to stop himself. It was too insulting. They were *overly sweet, brown balls of . . . urgh!* He shuddered at the thought of the ingredients. So, the haunting had had to wait.

But, inviting her, the enemy, to see 'real chocolat*'?* 'How could I have been so FOOLISH?'

He tried deep, calming breaths.

It didn't work.

Breathing was for the living! Old habits were just hard to break – which was why he still sometimes accidentally found himself floating on to the loo.

'*SACRÉ BLEU!*' he wailed. 'I don't even have any *chocolat.*'

Maybe he could find some?

But no. What was he thinking?

'I want them out of my Hôtel Framboise!'

16

To say that Coco hardly slept would be an understatement.

Once Mum and Dad had gone back to bed, she'd spent all night going over and over everything that had happened, her mind on overdrive and adrenaline coursing through her body.

The ghost wants to show me 'real' chocolate?
WHY would he do that?
What does that even mean?
Should I go?
What if it's a trap?
Could he be dangerous?
SO. MANY. QUESTIONS!

The clock hit 6.30 a.m. The sky streaked pink. It was too early to knock on Louis's door, but he'd not answered her texts and she'd explode if she didn't talk to him FAST.

He'd told her his room was at the back of their house, overlooking a tree, so she grabbed her cardigan and sneaked out of the hotel with Belle, dashing across the square and wiggling silently into his back garden through a gap in the wall. There was a glorious view of the lavender fields from here, unfurling below the sunrise in long purple ribbons, but Coco didn't notice . . . because there was the tree. The only one. With a big thick branch by a window . . . it had to be Louis's room.

'Stay, Belle,' she said. And without wasting a second, Coco found handholds and footholds in the gnarly trunk and branches to lift herself towards the big bough and Louis's window, leaving Belle to sit, dutifully, between two bumpy roots, watching her climb.

Coco reached the bough. *Now what?*

There was a gap of about two feet between her and the open window.

She could probably get a foot on the sill and, feeling like a burglar, she decided to do it. 'Don't look down!' she told herself. It was high and dangerous. She never would have done this in Burton-on-the-Bush. *Desperate times call for desperate measures*, she thought, as she held on tightly to an upper branch and carefully poked one foot off the bough. She stretched it on to the sill, then moved a hand across too . . .

There was Louis, fast asleep in his bed in the corner, next to a big illustrated book of *Les Trois Mousquetaires* by Alexandre Dumas (Dad had a copy too, so Coco knew it was *The Three Musketeers*). In another corner was his desk, covered with his drawings and pens and paints, and in the middle, on the floor, was his console, surrounded by scattered games boxes. It was a messy room, but nice!

Coco felt guilty about being there uninvited, so she knocked on the window. But Louis didn't stir, so she felt in her cardigan pockets for something to throw: *A paperclip . . . an old tissue . . . a spare poo bag . . . No.* Her fingers found the small roll of card from the Murder Cave. *That'll do*, she thought, and quickly screwed it into a ball.

'Uh!' It hit Louis smack on his forehead and bounced on to his duvet. He sat up, startled.

'Sorry!' whispered Coco, climbing down from the sill and tiptoeing over to the bed. She handed him his glasses, which were on the bedside table. 'It's only me.'

'C-Coco! What are you doing?' He switched on his bedside light.

'I climbed through the window,' she whispered.

'Through the win—?'

'Yes. Louis. Listen,' she said hurriedly. 'The Monsieur Framboise ghost, he came and I threw salt at him and . . .' She told him everything.

'I cannot believe it!' Louis whispered when she'd

finished. He thought for a moment, now very much awake. 'But I do not understand – why would a ghost say it wants to show you real chocolate, in the middle of a haunting?'

Coco shrugged. 'I dunno. When I told him he should eat the Nibby's, something changed. I sensed he was lonely. And then we heard Mum . . . Oh! I don't know. I hope it's not a trick. I mean, why does he want to meet in the wine cellar? Dad says there's nothing down there but empty wine crates and an old wooden cupboard.'

'You need to be really careful,' said Louis matter-of-factly. 'Scaring you. Breaking mirrors. Inviting you to discover "real" chocolate at midnight. In the WINE CELLAR – a classic, scary haunting ground . . . This ghost is unpredictable, which means he might be *dangereux*. I mean, who is to say he did not just make you think he was lonely, so you will do as he says?'

Coco hadn't thought of that.

'*Non*. The longer this haunting is going on, the worse it seems to be getting,' said Louis. 'I think you need to get rid of him, FAST! And not just for yourselves. Imagine what he will do when you have guests. He might scare them too, then no one will come.'

Coco gasped. She'd not thought about their future guests either. Louis was right. Haunting her family was bad enough, but if the ghost haunted everyone who came, the hotel would get a bad reputation and all her parents' hard work would have been for nothing.

'And salt clearly does not work,' added Louis.

'Unless you want to tickle him to death!' said Coco.

'Which would be difficult, because he is already dead!' Louis grinned.

Coco grinned back. 'So that just leaves – like you said – finding out his unfinished business.'

'Which means you must get to know him. I study flowers to know when they will bloom; you must study him to find out why he is still here.'

Coco looked at Louis. He was quite unlike any boy she'd ever met. 'Are you saying I'm going to have to meet him, then?'

'*Oui*,' whispered Louis with a flinch. 'I am sorry, but I think it is the only way.'

'OK. But you're coming with me.'

He looked ready to faint.

'Come on! You said it sounds dangerous. And I'm not going into a dark wine cellar by myself, at midnight, to meet a scary ghost.' She picked up the crumpled card she'd thrown earlier and threw it at him again. 'Come on!'

'What is this, anyway?' said Louis, unravelling it.

'Dunno,' said Coco. 'Belle was sniffing at it when we were in the Murder Cave.'

Louis carefully uncrumpled it to reveal flouncy

French handwriting – all swirls and curves. 'That is weird,' he said, scrutinizing the writing. 'It looks like a recipe. I think the title reads *Ganache, je t'aime!* "Ganache, I love you". I can see you need . . . dark chocolate, and I think that says "cream".'

'What? Let me see.' Coco leant over. She knew that ganache was a creamy chocolatey filling that you could put inside chocolate or pastries or use as icing. 'Why would a recipe for that be tucked away in the Murder Cave?'

Louis shrugged.

Coco examined the card some more, then gasped. There, in the top right-hand corner, were two faint blue letters – an 'H' and an 'F'.

'Louis, I think the recipe is from the hotel. Look. H and F – Hôtel Framboise. There was the same lettering on a chocolate pot Mum found.' She paused. 'What if making chocolate is his unfinished business?'

'Could be,' he replied. 'I mean, he is clearly a ghost chocolatier, who had a chocolate shop in the hotel – we say *chocolatier* for the chocolate maker and their shop in French,' he explained. 'He smells of chocolate when he is haunting you. And he wants to show you what "real *chocolat*" is.'

'So, will you come?' asked Coco.

Louis pulled a face. He looked terrified.

'You could take notes.' She pointed to his piles of notepads. 'I mean, you've been seeing Monsieur Framboise your whole life. This is your chance to *solve the mystery* too.'

'B-but what if it is a trick?' he stuttered.

'It might be,' said Coco. 'But he's had plenty of opportunities to push us down the stairs or drop things on our heads. And he hasn't done any of those things.'

'Yet!' said Louis. 'Maybe that is why he said to go to the cellar.'

'That's why you need to come with me,' said Coco.

Louis opened his mouth, but nothing came out. Then, after a moment, he said a squeaky, 'OK.'

'I knew it!' said Coco, punching the air. 'And we should show him this card. It's a recipe for chocolate ganache. If making chocolate is his unfinished business, then this will give him something to make.'

'But there is a problem,' said Louis.

'What?'

'Where is the ghost supposed to get ingredients from?'

'The spookermarket?' said Coco.

'The what market?' said Louis, confused.

'You know . . . a supermarket for ghosts. Spooker . . . Super . . .'

Louis looked at her blankly.

'Never mind.'

'No. We cannot leave details like the ingredients to chance,' Louis continued. 'If making chocolate is his unfinished business, we should bring them with us.' He looked at the card again. 'I think we have some chocolate and cream downstairs. I'll sneak them out.'

'Thanks, Louis!' Coco said, the ball in her stomach easing. 'I'm glad you're coming. I can't imagine what the ghost might do to me or my family if I don't go. And I really don't want to do this alone.'

'*De rien*,' said Louis, which Coco knew meant 'it's nothing' or 'no problem'.

It made them both blush, so the friends quickly looked up at the clock on Louis's wall, and saw it was already eight in the morning.

'Oh no! Mum and Dad will be wondering where I am!' Coco panicked.

'Let us head to the *boulangerie*,' Louis suggested. 'If you take some bread or pastries home, you can say you wanted to surprise them with breakfast. I will come too. I will leave a note for my parents. They will already be out in the fields by now,' he said. 'And if we are going to meet Monsieur Framboise, we need to check out your wine cellar first, while it is light. He said that room for a reason. We need to make sure there is no place he could hide, or worse, trap us in.'

*

Belle howled a scolding 'woo-woo-woo!' when she saw Coco trundle out of the back door with Louis.

'I know!' Coco cooed, rubbing Belle's head and kissing her nose. 'I'm sorry. I was gone a long time. Who's a good dog!'

Belle wagged her tail ferociously, instantly forgiving her.

Then the friends headed to the bakery, where Louis ordered a baguette for Coco.

'But you will have to learn to speak French one day,' he said.

'I know,' said Coco. 'How come your English is so good?'

'We have cousins in London, and go every Christmas. I like watching films and playing video games in English, too. You just have to practise.'

Coco sighed. *So everyone keeps telling me.*

Then they walked back up the hill, thinking up silly reasons for why Monsieur Framboise was still hanging around – 'His chocolates were so gooey they trapped his soul!' 'He lost his watch and can't tell it's time to go!' It felt good to laugh. It made the task ahead feel less impossible.

'Is that Madame Auguste?' said Coco, as they approached the square. An elderly lady with a walking stick was standing under a tree, staring at the hotel.

'That is weird,' Louis whispered. 'We never usually see her out here . . . *Bonjour, madame,*' he said politely, as they passed.

Madame Auguste swung round as if she'd been caught red-handed doing something bad. Then she scowled at the children and trundled back inside her house, without so much as a word.

Coco and Louis gave each other a knowing stare. Then they burst out laughing. She really was unpleasant.

'Look, Louis!' exclaimed Coco. There was a red sports car parked in front of the hotel. 'Isn't that the car we passed on our bikes yesterday?'

17

A well-dressed man got out of the driving seat as the children approached, his ear-length grey hair flopping over one side of his clean-shaven face. 'Oh, hello!' he said with an English accent. 'Is this the Hôtel Framboise?'

Coco made to say 'yes', but no words would come out, because . . . the man was none other than Atticus Carmichael! Celebrity chef and presenter of *Bake the Day*. Her, Kate and Rose's favourite TV baking show!

What on earth was he doing there?

She felt her heart speed up and her hands start to sweat.

'Ha, silly question!' Carmichael glanced up at the hotel name outside without waiting for a reply. 'I can see it is . . . and look . . .' He seemed very excited. 'There it is

– just like in the video. The "Chocolatier" sign!'

Hearing a stranger's voice, Mum and Dad stepped outside.

'Hello, how can we help y—' Mum stopped in her tracks. 'Oh my word! You're Atticus Carmichael!'

'Guilty as charged,' said the man, holding up his arms as if awaiting arrest. Then he smiled cheerily and shook Mum and Dad's hands.

'I can't believe it! I can't believe it!' said Coco to Louis.

'Me neither!' said Louis, just as wide-eyed. 'Mum has all his cookbooks.'

Belle, the only one who seemed unimpressed, sat down next to Coco.

'I'm Cheryl Bean. This is Burt, my husband, our daughter Coco – oh, that's where you were, at the bakery, thanks.' Mum took the baguette, trying to compose herself. 'And her friend, Louis. What brings you here, Mr Carmichael?'

'Well, you!' Carmichael said with a smile.

'Us?' said Dad. 'I don't understand.'

'You see, I'm here in France looking for ideas for a new TV show. I've always been interested in people who sell up and move abroad. It's not always easy to link that to food for a cooking programme, of course, but one of your posts, Madam Bean, popped into my feed – pun intended!' He laughed at his own joke. 'And I saw all the work you're doing at this charming hotel with its mysterious "Chocolatier" sign, and well . . . I've become rather obsessed.'

'Really?!' said Dad, staring in disbelief at Mum.

'Yes,' said Carmichael.

Mum had never looked so flattered.

'I do apologize for turning up unannounced, but I'd love to stay at the hotel, if that's OK?'

'Well, um, the guest rooms aren't rea—' Dad started, but it turned into a grunt as Mum elbowed him.

'We'd LOVE that!' she interjected.

Dad looked surprised, but backed her up. 'Erm . . . yes, of course. I'm sure we can sort something out. Though you'll have to share our bathroom. The . . . erm . . . guest plumbing's not finished yet.'

'Not a problem,' said Carmichael, warmly. 'I've roughed it in places less hospitable than this delightful spot.' He winked.

Coco couldn't believe her ears. Atticus Carmichael – *the* Atticus Carmichael, the famous TV chef, was about to stay at their hotel. He was the oldest of *Bake the Day*'s three presenters – a bit like an eccentric grandad, always wearing a white shirt and a colourful bowtie. But still very cool. Kate and Rose would be *so* jealous! This was so exciting!

'I'd love to get to know you all.' Carmichael smiled

kindly. His bowtie was red today. 'Maybe there's a programme idea I can sell to the BBC – with your permission, of course.'

'A TV renovation show. About the hotel. For the BBC?' squeaked Mum.

'If I can tie it in with food, yes,' said Carmichael.

Mum looked ready to faint with joy.

'I'll pay you for board and lodgings, of course. And, perhaps, you'll allow me to cook for you occasionally?' He moved to pat Belle, but she growled.

'Belle,' Coco said. 'Quiet. That's rude.'

'That sounds brilliant!' cried Mum again, with a silly giggle. 'We'd love to have you! And of course you can cook. How could we refuse a man with . . . how many cooking awards, again?'

'Oh, not that many,' said Carmichael. 'Only fifty-five!'

Mum eyed Dad as if to say, *This is what we've been waiting for! Can you believe our luck?*

And so it was decided, and everyone traipsed inside – Dad carrying Carmichael's suitcase into the lobby; Louis looking both excited and terrified to be in the hotel. He kept glancing around.

'Have you ever been inside before?' Coco whispered as they lingered in the hall, away from adult ears.

He shook his head.

'Is the ghost here now?' he whispered.

'I don't think so,' said Coco. 'Well, he must be somewhere, but . . . I can't sense him – which is good. This has to end tonight, Louis. With Carmichael here, we *really* can't risk anything bad happening.'

'Gosh, what a wonderful doer-upper you have!' Carmichael suddenly boomed, as he looked around the lobby. 'If I'd known this place was for sale, I might have bought it myself!'

Dad showed Atticus Carmichael to Guest Room 1 (it was the only one with wallpaper). Then Coco and Louis (Belle in tow) crept into the kitchen to get the wine cellar key – it had a big heavy lock. Coco found the key in the bits-and-bobs drawer and slipped it into her pocket. Then the friends tried to sneak unseen through the lobby to the cellar door. Louis was right. Why had the ghost told her to meet him there? They had to check it was safe before their midnight encounter. But . . .

It was impossible!

Every time they tried, Mum called Coco over to help 'tidy this' and 'tidy that'. She felt like Cinderella. Even Louis got roped in to putting some tools away.

Then Dad appeared in the kitchen, looking stressed. 'I've managed to put Carmichael's bed together,' he said, 'but he needs a plug adapter. I think our spare one is in a box somewhere, but I don't know where.'

'Shall we check the cellar?' Coco suggested, seizing the opportunity.

'No, thanks,' said Dad. 'There aren't any boxes there, and I don't want you two going down by yourselves.'

'Nice try,' whispered Louis.

Coco frowned.

After what felt like a thousand chores later, it was nearly lunchtime, and they'd still not made it down to the cellar.

'Do not panic,' Louis whispered. 'Maybe we will get a chance to go after lunch.' But then there came a knock at the door, and there were Louis's parents on the front step.

'*Bonjour*,' they said to Coco's parents. 'We got Louis's note, so we thought it was about time we came to say hello.'

'Oh, *bonjour*,' said Mum and Dad, doing the *bise* (that's greeting people with a kiss on each cheek, the French way – well, the air by their cheeks, not a proper smacker. It was a part of French culture and Coco wasn't sure she'd ever get used to it). They ushered Louis's parents into the kitchen to tell them all about Atticus Carmichael. Then, as if on cue (just as Louis's mum squeaked with excitement), in came Carmichael himself, booming, 'Don't worry! I found my adapter,' then, to Louis's parents,

'Oh, hello!' So, the cheek kissing started up again, and Mum and Dad asked everyone if they'd like to stay for lunch . . .

But then Mum opened the fridge door and realized they'd not got enough food. 'This is so embarrassing!' she said, holding up half a potato and a limp cucumber.

'Not at all. Not at all,' said Carmichael. 'I'm the one imposing, and I've got lots of lovely fresh market produce in the boot of my car. How about I do the cooking?'

And so, everyone stayed.

Which meant that although they ate a delicious meal – tomato and rosemary tart, *coq au vin* (chicken in red wine sauce), then the most delicious lemon meringue pie Coco had ever tasted – there was never a moment to check the cellar.

And like many traditional French meals, it went on for hours.

At four-thirty, they were all still at the table. (Coco had been sitting for so long now, her bum had gone to sleep!) Then Carmichael whipped up a strawberry cheesecake for teatime. And by then it was more or less time for dinner – bread, cheese and poached pears – all prepared by Carmichael while he quizzed Mum and Dad about what they'd found in the hotel – Mum looked for the chocolate pot to show him, but couldn't find it – before regaling them with stories of his time as a junior chef.

'Oh, I hardly knew an apple from an orange when I was younger!' he laughed, as they were just finishing dinner. 'Once, I went to the kitchen garden for some mint leaves, but came back with grass. And another time, for an official meal at the British Embassy in Paris, I added too much nutmeg to some spiced bread. It's a tricky spice, nutmeg – too little and there's no flavour; too much and it can cause hallucinations . . . Let's just say that the French Minister thought her dinner partner, the British Ambassador, was a giant sausage!'

'Well, I'm glad you told us this after the meal,' laughed Louis's mum. 'Or we might not have stayed. And that would have been a shame,' she added earnestly, 'because it was truly delicious. And' – she turned to Coco's parents – 'we've had a wonderful time! *Merci!* But *oh là là!*' She looked at the clock on her phone. 'It's ten-thirty. We should go.'

Coco began to panic. She couldn't believe they'd been stuck there all day! The ghost would be there soon, and they'd still not seen the cellar!

Worse, the kitchen was such a mess, Mum and Dad would probably be up for hours past midnight cleaning up.

Louis was panicking too. 'I have to go,' he said. 'We cannot do anything about the cellar now. But I will be back soon – in time for you know what. Just make sure the coast is clear.'

The grown-ups gave each other the *bises* goodbye, then Carmichael announced that he was going to bed. 'Toodle-oo!' he said with a bow (his signature move at the end of every *Bake the Day* episode), then up the stairs he went.

And for a moment – after a whirlwind of a day and with a long night to come – Coco was relieved to find herself alone with Mum, Dad and Belle in the kitchen just like a normal evening. Well, apart from the mess . . . and her midnight rendezvous with the ghost . . . and the ball of fear filling her stomach.

'It looks like Carmichael got everything out of every cupboard,' Coco said, looking at the piles of plates and mixers and knives and cutting boards, and trying to sound calm.

'Well, I suppose he's used to having lots of staff,' said Mum. 'They probably do all the tidying.'

Coco looked urgently at the clock.

Only an hour until ghost time, and she'd never be able to go if they stayed up to tidy.

She had to act now. 'Mum, Dad, you both look so tired,' she said.

'We are,' said Dad.

'Well, why don't we all go to bed. We can do this in the morning. I can get up early and load the dishwasher, then help with the rest.'

'Oh, sweetheart! You're always so helpful!' said Mum. 'It's a great idea! But there's no need for you to get up. You need your sleep, too. We'll do it.'

'OK,' said Coco.

Dad hugged her goodnight.

Phew! That had been easier than she'd thought. 'I'll let Belle out, then I'll go up!' she shouted as her parents headed upstairs.

She patted her pocket. The key was still there. *Now everyone just needs to fall asleep. FAST.*

19

'Did you get out OK?' Coco whispered to Louis as she opened the front door at two minutes to midnight. He was holding a triple pack of seventy per cent dark chocolate and a big pot of cream. Belle was pleased to see him. She licked his cheek.

'Yes,' said Louis. 'Though Maman got up for a glass of water, so I had to wait.' His voice sounded normal, but Coco could sense he was scared.

She was too.

'Mum and Dad are definitely asleep,' she whispered. She could make out their snoring slicing slowly through the quiet. 'But I don't know about Carmichael, so we'd better be extra quiet.'

Hearts racing, the friends tiptoed through the lobby towards the wine cellar door. Coco's palms were sweating more than when she tried to speak French, and Louis said his knees were wobbly. Even Belle had her tail between her legs.

Would Monsieur Framboise try to drop something on their heads?

Or would he really try to tell them about real chocolate?

Was there anywhere he could hide?

Or trap them in?

There was only one way to find out!

Coco took a deep breath, drew the key from her pocket, then tried it in the lock.

It was old and stiff, but after a rusty click the door swung outwards to reveal a dark, dusty staircase.

Light from the lobby flooded down it, warping the friends' shadows into long shapes, like human and dog accordions folding down the steps.

'Here goes,' said Coco, patting her pocket, which she'd filled with salt.

Louis clutched the ingredients tightly to his chest and nodded.

Then down the stairs they went.

Coco thought her heart would burst out of her chest. It was one thing being haunted; it was quite another walking willingly into an unfamiliar cellar to meet the spook. She closed the door behind them, keeping her phone torch stretched out in front of them as they went, bracing herself for a fight.

THERE WAS THE GHOST! Floating just below the ceiling, his body translucent and his round, moustachioed face glaring at them through icy blue eyes.

Louis's mouth dropped open. It was the face he'd been seeing for years – only this time it was up close and attached to a body, dressed like a chef.

'*GROOUW,*' squeaked Belle, her head tilted to one side.

'RRRRRAAAAA!' roared the ghost, stretching out his arms and suddenly doubling in size like a balloon, almost filling the whole cellar. 'GET OUT OF MY HOTEL!' he bellowed. And it was terrifying . . .

Well, to Louis. He cringed in the corner behind Belle, who let out a whine.

To Coco, though, it pushed a different button – her anger button. ENOUGH WAS ENOUGH! She was sick and tired of this ghost and his theatrics. If making chocolate was his unfinished business, by hook or by crook, she was going to make sure he made it. TONIGHT! Because she wanted him GONE! VANISHED! DEPARTED! Out of her and Mum's and Dad's – but especially now, Carmichael's – way.

'You brought me to a dank wine cellar to tell me that?' She sounded braver than she felt.

The ghost stopped in his tracks. He was so surprised,

he just floated there for a moment, flickering in and out of focus. Why wasn't she running away? 'B-b-but . . .' he blubbed.

'But what, Isidore Framboise? You told us to come. And now you're trying to scare us by being all shouty and huge! Do you know what I think? I think you're rude!'

'Rude? I am not rude!' he retorted. '*You* are rude! It is you who moved into my home, without asking!'

'But we bought it fair and square. And you're dead.'

'I am not dead.'

'You *are* dead! You're a ghost!'

A weird mist began seeping out from under Monsieur Framboise's chef's hat, as if he were boiling up inside. Louis backed away towards the cellar steps, ready to run any second!

'You'd better start behaving, Monsieur Framboise,' Coco continued, shouting up to the ceiling. 'We have a paying guest! A famous TV chef! Atticus Carmichael.'

'That bowtied buffoon is famous?'

'Yes.'

'Well, I've never heard of him. Anyway. Why is he here? You and your family are destroying the hotel!' the ghost shouted down.

'No, we are not! My mum and dad have sunk everything we own into doing up this wreck. And if we're not up and running by Easter, we're ruined, and this place will end up falling down. You should be grateful we're here!'

Louis gulped.

Belle curled into a ball.

Coco felt so angry, she wanted to throw the ingredients at Monsieur Framboise, but she knew she had to stay on track. If they were going to end this and find his unfinished business, they needed to get him to make the recipe.

'Anyway, you told me you'd show me "what real chocolate is", so there's someone I want you to meet. My friend Louis.' She nudged Louis, who was clutching the ingredients like weapons. 'He has brought you some things . . .'

Monsieur Framboise looked up as if noticing there was someone else in the room for the first time. He sniffed the air. 'You brought *chocolat* and cream?'

Louis nodded, his mouth wide.

Monsieur Framboise floated down from the ceiling, deflating to his normal size.

'You are that boy I've seen looking at me!' he said, pointing his finger straight into Louis's shoulder.

Then both of them looked shocked: Louis, because he'd felt a cold tingle whoosh down his arm and up his neck; Monsieur Framboise, because he'd forgotten he could feel people's emotions when he touched them, and now he knew Louis was both terrified and fascinated, and both excited to be there and wishing he were back home in the safety of his own room – all at the same time!

'And look, Monsieur Framboise,' said Coco, sensing they'd caught the ghost's attention. 'We found this too. Is it yours?' She eyed Louis, who slowly, shakily, drew the recipe card from his pocket and moved it towards the ghost.

'Where did you get this?' asked Monsieur Framboise. He looked like he'd seen a ghost himself.

'In the Murder Cave,' said Coco.

'The *what* cave?' Monsieur Framboise's moustache wiggled as he said the word 'cave'.

'*La Grotte Meurtrière*,' Louis managed to utter despite his still-obvious terror. It was the French name. 'In th-the hillside.'

Monsieur Framboise didn't take the card, but rather shoved his face into it, then, as if it were the most natural thing in the world, announced, 'Aah, my *Ganache, je t'aime*. It is a recipe *extraordinaire*!'

He extracted his face, and – as if the hauntings of the last few weeks had never taken place and meeting the children in a dark, dank wine cellar at midnight was the most normal thing in the world – he said, 'Come on, then.'

'Come on then, where?' said Coco, warily. She still

wasn't sure they could trust him.

'You brought *chocolat* and cream, didn't you?' said Monsieur Framboise. 'So we will do the recipe.'

Coco looked around at the dusty floor and empty wine crates. 'In here?' she said suspiciously.

'*Non!*' said Monsieur Framboise. 'In here . . .' The ghost turned to the wooden wine cupboard. 'Open it.'

Coco pulled the doors wide open. 'But it's just a cupboard,' she said, peering in.

Belle sniffed the back panel.

'Really?' said Monsieur Framboise, illuminating the space with his iridescent glow, and pointing to a little lever at the back. 'Pull that,' he said to Louis.

Louis did as he was told, and – *CLICK!*

The back panel opened into a narrow passageway, with a stone staircase leading down.

'Come,' said Monsieur Framboise, floating into the darkness.

After three steps, the stones became uneven, as if thousands of feet had worn the central sections away. They felt ancient – like they belonged to an old dungeon.

And that's because they did!

'This used to be part of Château Mont-Lavande,' announced Monsieur Framboise. 'It was once an *oubliette*.'

Coco remembered what the library book said. That the village was built on top of where the castle once stood. 'Isn't that where they used to put people, then just forget about them?' Coco exclaimed, suddenly feeling nervous.

'*Oui!*' said Monsieur Framboise. 'Hurry now!'

'I hope he is not going to lock us in,' whispered Louis.

'Me too,' said Coco.

They stopped, and Monsieur Framboise floated to one side of the passageway to illuminate a handle hanging from a cord.

When Coco pulled it, an old, dusty lightbulb spluttered on to reveal – *Phew!* – not an *oubliette*, but the most magnificent chocolate-making workshop anyone had ever seen – all wooden panels with white and blue porcelain tiles, and shining marble surfaces, and a whole host of copper pots and other apparatus. Everything was spick and span, as if it were new. In fact, only the vaulted ceiling gave any hint that the room had once been a dungeon.

'Wow!' said Louis. 'Papa would love to make our jam in here!'

'*Fantastique, non?*' said Monsieur Framboise, with a glint in his eye. 'I built this in secret. Almost no one knew it was here! The temperature underground is stable, so it is *parfait* – perfect – for making little chocolate treasures.'

'How is it so clean?' Coco said.

'Because once a chocolatier, always a chocolatier!' announced Monsieur Framboise proudly. 'A chocolatier must always be ready with a clean, organized space. I had always secretly hoped I would make chocolate again – though I did not think it possible – so I have put almost all of my spectral energy – *c'est de l'énergie spectrale, Louis* – into keeping it clean. *Almost* all. The rest I put into haunting you, Mademoiselle Bean.' He raised his eyebrows. 'But for tonight, at least, I shall put it into the recipe.'

Belle let out a grumbling woof, and Monsieur Framboise turned to face her.

'Keep an eye on the door? Yes, Belle, good idea,' he said.

Belle immediately trotted over to the door and lay down, her eyes fixed on the stairs.

'Y-you know what she's thinking? And that she is called Belle?' Coco's mouth hung open.

'*Oui*, when you are dead, it is easier to communicate with animals.'

'What is she thinking now?' said Coco, wide-eyed.

'That the floor is nice and cool . . . and – *oui, ça c'est sûr, Belle* – that she mustn't eat the chocolate, as it is poisonous for dogs!'

Coco and Louis just stood there, stunned . . . until Monsieur Framboise snapped them out of it by asking for the ingredients and the card. Louis, still wide-eyed, placed them on the marble counter.

'So, Coco, to melt chocolate we need a . . . ?'

'Saucepan?' she answered, still not quite believing this was happening.

'And . . . ?'

'Erm . . . a spoon?'

'Yes, but you also need a bowl to make a bain-marie.' (Which sounded like the name 'Anne-Marie', but with a 'B'.)

'W-what is a bain-marie?' Louis asked nervously.

Monsieur Framboise opened his mouth to reply, but it was Coco who dared to speak first: 'You put boiling water in the saucepan, then a bowl on top of that, then you put the chocolate in the bowl. The steam melts the chocolate.'

'*Exactement!*' said Monsieur Framboise, a smile flickering underneath his moustache, just for a moment, before he stifled it. 'A bain-mariiiiiiie,' he continued, as though tasting the word when he spoke it, 'is a chocolatier's best friend. It is like a Jacuzzi for the *chocolat*! It gives better heat control when you are melting. Now, open one of the packets of *chocolat*.'

Coco took off the wrapper, though she didn't know whether she should stay, run or shout for Mum and Dad. The ghost, though not exactly friendly, was now acting so much like a – well, a normal person. It was strange. His loneliness was still there, too, and Coco wondered if he'd been feeling it since 1981, when he'd died. Maybe even longer? She'd been lonely ever since she'd arrived in France and it wasn't nice. She couldn't imagine feeling that way for so many years. She suddenly felt sorry for him.

Monsieur Framboise sniffed the chocolate deeply. 'Seventy per cent *cacao*, is it not?'

'Impressive,' Coco found herself saying.

The ghost smiled proudly. 'The ears of great musicians have perfect pitch. The noses of great chocolatiers have perfect *cacao* detection. Now, Louis, for *Ganache, je t'aime* we need some heart-shaped moulds and a paintbrush.'

'A paintbrush?'

'I mean . . . pastry brush. They are over there on the shelf in the pantry.'

Louis walked over to the pantry with a new-found grin on his face. Since he'd realized Monsieur Framboise wasn't going to hurt them, he was enjoying himself. It wasn't every day you got to make chocolate with a ghost chef, who spoke to animals, in a secret workshop built in an ancient *oubliette*!

Coco dropped the chocolate into the bain-marie on the old gas cooker (miraculously still working).

'Good, now stir it to the rhythm of your heartbeat,' said Monsieur Framboise.

Coco smiled sheepishly. 'My heartbeat?' she said. That sounded silly.

'*Oui, oui,*' said Monsieur Framboise. He was very serious. 'Ingredients count. But what turns simple *chocolat* into extraordinary *chocolat* is this.' He beat gently on his chest with one hand – 'Boum-boum, boum-boum' – and did a stirring movement mid-air with the other. 'Never underestimate the magic of your heart. Some would call it love.'

'Love?'

'Yes. And it is my special ingredient.'

Coco looked at Louis wide-eyed, not knowing what to think, but she started stirring anyway. Some people would say cooking with a ghost chef was impossible, and yet here she was. Who was to say that adding love to chocolate was silly?

'Now, Louis . . .' Monsieur Framboise floated over to his side. 'Time to make the hearts. You brush the bottom of the moulds with *chocolat*, like this, then spread it up the sides.' He guided Louis and the pastry brush. 'Good. Now, we leave them to cool. Then we repeat four times.'

Monsieur Framboise turned to Coco. 'Now, for the ganache.'

'OK,' said Coco, grabbing the cream and a second packet of chocolate.

'For this you must finely chop the *chocolat*,' said Monsieur Framboise. 'There is a knife in there.' He pointed to a drawer below the work surface. 'And use a clean bowl for the bain-marie.'

Coco did as she was told, then dropped the chopped chocolate into the bowl.

'*Formidable!* Now, melt it like before, but . . . *tsk, tsk, tsk*!' He wagged a transparent finger at Coco as she reached for a spoon. 'But do not stir, this time. It already has the love it needs, and for the best ganache, we must not disturb the melting.'

Coco and Louis watched Monsieur Framboise hovering over the bowl as the chocolate melted. Then after a moment, he screwed up his eyes and said:

'*Bien*. Now, take the bowl off the heat and add the cream . . . *Oui, comme ça*. And now you can mix it, Coco.'

Coco immediately started whisking the cream into the melted chocolate until it was a creamy paste. It took several minutes.

Then, Monsieur Framboise peered into the bowl again and nodded. 'Good. Louis, how are our hearts?'

'Hard.'

'*Parfait.* Time to spoon in our ganache.'

Then, as if by magic, a teaspoon and the cooled bowl of ganache rose into the air and floated over to the moulds, where little blobs of lovely chocolatey cream dropped into each shape. Almost in the same movement, the still-warm bowl of leftover chocolate rose too, and poured its contents into each mould to seal the ganache inside.

'Objects moving on their own . . . he is a poltergeist!' whispered Louis.

Coco just nodded, too mesmerized to talk.

They waited in silence for the chocolates to cool, before turning them out of the moulds. They looked pretty. And it was strange, because for a split second, making the *Ganache, je t'aime* with Monsieur Framboise and Louis felt a bit like doing a class at Choco-Yum-Yums with her friends.

'All done!' said Monsieur Framboise, placing the chocolates on an old plate with the hotel initials on it and pocketing the recipe.

And that's when it happened.

A bright light started to glow around his head, and he looked stunned – as if in a trance.

'Coco, look! It is happening,' whispered Louis in wonder. 'We were right – making chocolate is his unfinished business. I think he is about to move on!'

Coco watched with wide eyes. They'd done it! Monsieur Framboise looked distant and ready to disappear! But . . .

'I remember now,' he whispered, still very much earthbound. 'I hid this recipe card there! There, where Madeleine and I . . .' He trailed off.

Madeleine?

Coco and Louis stared at each other. Monsieur Framboise wasn't moving on, he was having a memory . . .

Louis quickly got out his notepad and nudged Coco. *Ask him!* he mouthed.

'Why did you hide it there?' said Coco.

'I think . . .' said Monsieur Framboise, dreamily. 'I think . . . it was because . . .'

Coco and Louis leant towards him.

'*Non. Non.* I can't remember! But there was a reason . . . and . . . there are more of them . . .'

'More chocolate recipe cards like this?' said Coco. 'Where?'

'The place where the dead go,' said Monsieur Framboise. 'Forever!'

His face suddenly froze into a look of horror.

Coco gulped.

Then his body stiffened and he began to fade – leaving only his voice to echo through the air like a spooky radio. 'I remember now,' he howled. 'I WAS MURDERED!'

21

'He was murdered!' said Coco as they got back to the kitchen, hardly believing the words were coming out of her mouth. 'This is horrible!'

Louis had heard his death had been bad, but MURDER?

Louis looked pale.

Belle whined.

Coco felt stunned. In the last hour, they'd fought a ghost. Made chocolate with him. Learnt his special technique. Found out he could communicate with Belle. Discovered he'd hidden recipe cards, the first of which they'd found in a place he'd gone with a certain 'Madeleine'. Who was this Madeleine? And why would he have done that? The card seemed to have jogged his memory of her, and of being murdered.

Coco put the plate of chocolates on the only bit of kitchen table not smothered in dirty plates; she'd hide them in her room when she went to bed. Belle went to her basket. 'I hate to think someone was murdered in our home,' Coco said. 'It makes me feel icky. Like I'm not safe.'

'It was a long time ago, Coco. I am sure the murderer is long gone,' said Louis.

Without thinking, Coco shoved a chocolate into her mouth. Louis did too.

And it was an explosion of deliciousness on their tongues, coating every taste bud with creamy sweetness. They'd never tasted anything like it. The heartbeats had worked.

And eating them now, tasting the magic, made her realize something else too.

Monsieur Framboise was more than just a ghost. He'd been a real person once, with real feelings. She suddenly wanted to help him.

'We thought making chocolate was his unfinished business,' Louis said. 'But he is still here, so it cannot be. Now we know he was murdered – do you think it might be that? That he needs to solve the crime to move on?'

Coco gulped. 'Maybe. But how are we supposed to do that?!'

'By finding the other cards and making the recipes?'

said Louis. 'Parts of his memory came back when we had finished the chocolates, and he had put the recipe in his pocket. Perhaps if we find them all, he will remember everything?'

'I think you're right,' said Coco. 'But we should sleep on it. It's too much to take in after such a long day!'

Louis agreed.

So carefully, silently, making sure the coast was clear, Louis left through the front door, Coco kissed Belle goodnight, and everyone went to bed, unease pounding in their chests.

22

'AAAARRGGH!!!!!!!!!!!!!!!!!!!!!!!!'

It was Mum screaming, in the kitchen.

'Is everything all right?' shouted Coco, bursting in, half expecting Monsieur Framboise to have appeared in front of her parents. Or worse, in front of Atticus Carmichael.

'I don't believe it! I don't believe it!' Mum shrieked.

'Don't believe what?' said Coco.

Dad pointed at Mum's screen and Coco thought she'd faint. There on Mum's Hôtel Framboise page was a video of the *Ganache, je t'aime* chocolates, and just in front, on the table where Coco had left them, were the real ones!

Her heart began to race. How could she have been so stupid? How could she have forgotten to take them upstairs? More importantly, how was she going to explain? She couldn't let on about the ghost or the secret workshop.

'Your dad and I got up early to start cleaning,' Mum continued, a little breathless. 'We found the chocolates. I thought they were so pretty and delicious that I made a video of them, explaining how Carmichael is staying here and . . . it's had twelve thousand likes!' She pointed to the page.

'We've had nearly five hundred new followers in two hours!' added Dad. 'The "Chocolatier" sign video got hits. I mean, it's what caught Atticus's attention. But this! Wow!'

Coco's stomach fluttered.

'And look!' Mum clicked to see the list of likes. 'One like is from Nibby's – you know, the chocolate company!'

Of course Coco knew. Their chocolates had been whizzing across her room!

'Is everything all right down here? I heard screaming!' Carmichael hurried in wearing striped purple silk pyjamas, a yellow silk dressing gown and brown suede slippers – *like funny camouflage for the fields outside*, Coco thought.

'Oh, you wonderful, wonderful man!' Mum rushed over to shake his hand. 'We're more than all right. Thank you! They're fabulous!'

'What are fabulous?' said Carmichael, confused, but

shaking her hand anyway.

'The chocolates.'

Coco gasped. Mum thought it was Carmichael!

'What chocolates?'

'The surprise chocolates you left out for us.' Mum pointed at the plate and the computer screen.

'Oh, gosh. This is embarrassing. I didn't leave them,' Carmichael said apologetically. 'Though' – he picked up the plate to examine them – 'these are extraordinarily good-looking. I wonder who did?'

Coco squirmed on the spot. What should she do? There was no one else it could have been except her. She'd have to make up a story. 'I-I did,' she squeaked. 'I made them with Louis . . . at his house,' she lied. 'A couple of days ago. I wanted to surprise you.'

'*You* made them?' said Mum, shocked.

'Yes,' said Coco.

'With Louis?'

'Yes.'

'And it is your own recipe?' Carmichael asked, examining the plate.

'Yes!' Coco replied, trying not to blink or look away. Because what else could she say? She couldn't say she'd got it from a ghost.

'And on a Hôtel Framboise plate too! How lovely!'

Mum did a double take. In the excitement, she'd not

noticed the plate. 'Where did you find that?'

'In my room,' Coco said quickly. 'Behind the bed!'

'Well, I think I should taste one,' said Carmichael, popping one into his mouth, whole.

'I'll have another one,' said Mum, picking up two.

'And me!' said Dad. 'I've rarely tasted anything so lovely.'

'Extraordinary!' said Carmichael. He looked excited. 'A fine shell and such succulent ganache. If you were on my TV show, you'd win with these. You must give me the recipe!'

Coco squirmed. The recipe wasn't hers to give. It belonged to Monsieur Framboise.

'Coco, I'm so proud of you,' Mum declared. 'Those classes at Choco-Yum-Yums have clearly paid off!'

'They most certainly have,' said Carmichael. 'You'd better have more recipes up your sleeve, young lady, because you have a gift. As a chef, I recognize culinary flair when I see it.'

Mum swelled with pride. Then her computer pinged.

'Gosh, look! We've just had ten more follows. And a hundred and seven likes. It'll be hard to match this video with any others,' she said, suddenly looking stressed.

And Coco recognized the look. It was a 'we need more money if we're to open by Easter' look. Mum needed to be a real influencer to make this work.

'Well, I'll gladly repost your videos, Cheryl,' said Carmichael, strolling over to the end of the table, where Dad had laid out his breakfast – croissants and fruit salad. 'I have over a million followers. I'm sure you'll get many more likes. The world needs to know about Coco's chocs.'

'You'd do that?'

'Of course!' said Carmichael, drawing out his phone and typing something. 'I've just done this one now.'

Mum was so happy she rushed over to hug him.

Carmichael laughed and hugged her back.

Coco smiled, a wave of relief sweeping over her. She'd got away with it. She felt guilty for lying, but what choice had she had? She looked at Mum and Dad – for a moment their worries seemed to have melted away.

23

ROSE
OMG. Me and Kate wish we'd made those chocs with you. They're so pretty. ☺ ☺ ☺

KATE
Can you believe it! Carmichael said, 'They taste so good, I'm almost jealous!!!!!!!' Coco, you're a star ☺

ROSE
Mum says can you get his autograph?

Since Carmichael's repost, the kitchen had been awash with pinging – and not just because of Coco's friends' texts. People from far and wide had been commenting on Mum's video, complimenting the chocolates.

They're magic!
So pretty!
Give us a taste! Ha!

In less than an hour, she had fifteen thousand more followers and the video had been liked more than seventy thousand times! It was as if the chocolates (and Carmichael's TV chef account) contained magic.

The chocolates really do, thought Coco, putting her hand to her heart and listening to its beat.

And all this had given her an idea.

'Monsieur Framboise, Monsieur Framboise,' she and Louis called into the attic room later that morning. They realized he'd left so abruptly the night before, they didn't know how to find him.

'It's here that he's appeared the most,' said Coco. 'So hopefully he'll hear us. We really need to talk.'

But nothing.

'Maybe he is in his workshop,' suggested Louis.

So, making sure the coast was clear, they unlocked the wine cellar and crept down into his secret workshop – as tidy now as when they'd first laid eyes on it.

But a cold silence reigned, broken only by their trainers squeaking on the old flagstone floor. In fact, it felt rather spooky without him – which Coco pointed out was bizarre, as it was usually the presence of ghosts that made things feel frightening, rather than them *not* being there.

After lunch, they carried on the search. Mum and Dad had decided to do some tidying for Carmichael, and showed up sweeping, dusting and scrubbing almost everywhere they went.

Then, just when they thought they'd lost them, there was Carmichael too, scribbling notes – in the garden, in the future breakfast room, in the kitchen – and filming parts of the renovations with his phone.

'Don't forget to give me the recipe, kids!' he said with a smile. 'For the programme idea.'

'We won't,' said Coco, squirming. She didn't want to disappoint their famous guest. But the recipe really wasn't hers to give – and anyway, Monsieur Framboise had taken it back last night.

By two o'clock, she and Louis started to worry. Where was the ghost? The atmosphere felt light and warm, and the only things Belle had wagged at were normal, visible living-breathing humans and wall lizards scurrying up and down the purple wisteria at the back of the hotel.

Coco and Louis tried all the guest rooms. They even sneaked their heads into Carmichael's room. It was so messy it was as though he'd turned the place upside down! But still NOTHING!

Then she, Louis and Belle walked all around the outside of the hotel to see if Monsieur Framboise was there.

Carmichael was drinking wine at a table Dad had set up in the front garden by the gate, and strangely, Madame Auguste was on the square again, her eyes fixed on him.

'I bet she's a Carmichael fan,' said Coco, 'but too shy to go over.'

'Maybe,' said Louis.

By late afternoon, Coco didn't even feel like she was being watched any more. No matter where she went, it was as though the hotel was empty.

'Maybe his unfinished business was making chocolates one last time after all,' said Louis, after they'd retreated to Coco's bedroom. 'Maybe he is gone?'

'Maybe,' said Coco. 'But I have a feeling he's still— What's that?' she whispered. There was a loud sniffing noise coming from above them.

'It sounds like it is in the – how do you call them? – rafters,' said Louis, looking up at the ceiling.

Even though Coco's room was in the attic, there was still a small space above her ceiling filled with the wooden beams holding up the roof. There was a ladder next to her door that led up to a trapdoor in the ceiling.

'I think it is an animal,' said Louis. 'We had bats in our roof once and it sounded like that.'

'WAHH! WAHH-AHAHH!'

'Not bats,' Coco whispered. 'Monsieur Framboise! Come on.'

Peering in from the top of the ladder, both children thought they'd jump out of their skins. Sure enough, there was the ghost – perched on a wooden beam in the darkness. And what a mess he was in. Tears of ectoplasm were rolling down his face, collecting in shimmering glops on his moustache.

'Monsieur Framboise?' said Coco. 'What are you doing up here? We've been looking for you everywhere.'

'You don't know what it's like,' he blubbed.

'Don't know what what's like?' said Coco. 'Please don't cry loudly, Monsieur Framboise. The grown-ups might hear.'

'Let them hear,' came the loud, sniffy reply. 'I don't care any more. AHOUUUUUUUUUU!'

'I care,' said Coco. 'Please, be quiet, Monsieur Framboise! Come down into my room and we can talk there – quietly.'

'AHOUUUUUUUUUUU! WAHH!'

'SSSHT! Monsieur Framboise. Please!' Coco felt herself getting angry. She had to get him under control.

'Stop that this second. Come down into my room, now.' She was sounding rather like Mum.

But it worked.

Before she and Louis could so much as climb down from the top rung, Monsieur Framboise had plopped straight through the floor, bottom first, to sit hunched on the end of Coco's bed, his white chef's hat flopping over his eyes. He looked very sorry for himself.

'That's better,' said Coco, feeling like the grown-up.

Louis tried a supportive 'there-there' pat on Monsieur Framboise's arm, but his hand went straight through and he got another cold shiver.

'Now, why are you crying?' Coco said.

'B-because I was m-murdered. And I don't know why, or who did it,' he sniffed. 'Because I've been d-dead more years than I was alive. Because first my life was taken, then you moved in and now the hotel has been taken too!'

Coco gulped. She'd never thought of it like that.

'Because mice run through my toes,' he continued, just as a mouse scampered along the floor and through his foot. 'And because when you brought that recipe card and we made the *chocolat*, I remembered what it was like to be alive. WAHH! WAHH AHAHH! . . . I'm so lonely! I miss life. But at the same time, I want peace. Oh, I'm a mess! I don't know what to DOOOOOOOOOOO!'

Gosh, that was a lot of good reasons to cry, but . . .
'SHHHH!' Coco needed him to stop. 'We know you're terribly upset, but that's why we're here.'

'Monsieur Framboise,' said Louis, backing her up. 'Everyone says ghosts have unfinished business. You must have something left to finish on this earth. That is why you are still here. We think yours has something to do with your murder.'

'That recipe card jogged your memory,' said Coco. 'You said there are others. Maybe if we find them all, you will remember what happened? And maybe knowing that will help you, you know, find peace.'

'Maybe,' said Monsieur Framboise, looking hopeful for the first time.

This was it – what she wanted to talk to him about. She braced herself. 'And as strange as it is for me to say this,' said Coco, 'I actually think we can help each other.'

'What do you mean?' said Monsieur Framboise.

'Well, those chocolates we made – I'll explain how later, but they really helped my parents. And me and Louis enjoyed making them. And you looked like you did too. You said yourself that it made you feel alive again. What if you teach us how to make the chocolates on each recipe card we find?'

'You'd be my pupils? My apprentices?'

'It would be better than haunting us, wouldn't it?'

'B-but haunting, protecting the hotel, it is my duty!'

'Well, that's just silly,' said Coco. 'Haunting people isn't very nice. You should be concentrating on why you're still here, instead. If your soul needs to move on, you need to help it move on.'

Monsieur Framboise made to speak, then closed his mouth again.

'You have something left to do on this earth,' said Coco. 'Help us make chocolates so Mum can post videos of them, and we'll help you work out what happened to you.'

Monsieur Framboise thought for a second. 'Why would your mother post videos of the *chocolats*?' he said, confused. 'Where would she send them?'

And Coco realized that, as Monsieur Framboise hadn't left the hotel in over forty years, to post something still meant a postal service 'post' to him, like a letter. He didn't know what a mobile phone was or a social media post or probably even the internet.

'Like I said, I'll explain later,' Coco said. 'Teach us what you know, and we'll help you find the missing recipe cards. You love this hotel, don't you?'

'*Oui.*'

'Well, it would be your way of helping it. Because . . . as you've probably noticed, my mum and dad need all the help they can get.'

Monsieur Framboise was still for a moment, then conjured a handkerchief from his jacket pocket and wiped away his gloopy tears of ectoplasm.

'Let's do it. *Ça marche!*'

The next day, Louis arrived early. They headed straight to the attic bedroom, where Monsieur Framboise was waiting by the window.

'OK. If we are going to find the cards,' said Louis, sitting next to Coco on her bed, 'we need to work out where you might have put them.' He got out his notebook.

Coco watched Louis frowning behind his glasses and nibbling his pencil as if preparing for a big interrogation. Her friend would make a good detective, she thought.

'Can you remember anything about your life? *Par exemple*, what was a typical day for you? What would you do? Where would you go?' he said.

'Well, it is hard to remember,' said Monsieur Framboise. 'But I would wake up, and go to the *toilettes*—'

'Not that part,' Coco giggled. Louis too. 'Unless you

think you've hidden a card in the loo!'

'*Oh, non, non, non! Toilettes* are no places for recipes. How could you think such a thing?' Monsieur Framboise looked shocked at the mere suggestion. 'Then I would prepare breakfast in the kitchen. A fine breakfast of fresh bread and croissants and pains au chocolat and hot *chocolat* and coffee and fruits and,' he turned to Louis, 'your family's honey and lavender jam. Your grandmother made the finest lavender jam I ever tasted.'

'You knew her?' said Louis. 'She died before I was born.'

'Oh yes! Kind lady. I often hoped she had stayed behind as a ghost, but I sensed that she had moved on. Lucky *madame*! I am the only ghost in the village.'

Louis smiled.

'Then I would serve the breakfast in the garden, by the roses and raspberries. Then I would check out the guests who were leaving. Then clean the rooms. And welcome the new guests . . . and then, in the afternoon, I would make chocolate to sell in the shop, which was in the room at the back – where your parents want to put the breakfast room, Coco.'

'Did you do all this alone?' asked Coco. It sounded like a lot of hard work.

'No, sometimes Madeleine would help.' And the moment he said the name, he looked sad again.

'Madeleine?' said Louis. 'Who is she?' This was the second time her name had come up.

'Nobody,' the ghost said, suddenly looking as though he was in a daze. 'I don't want to talk about her.'

'OK,' said Coco, eyeing Louis, as if to say, *We need to find out more about that.* 'So, what else? Is there anywhere special to you where you might have hidden a recipe card?'

Monsieur Framboise thought for a second. 'Here, in the bedroom, maybe? My workshop? The pantry?'

They had a good look around Coco's attic bedroom, but didn't find anything.

Then they sneaked back through the wine cellar door to the workshop (narrowly missing Carmichael, who was sauntering through the lobby with his notebook), and found nothing there. And it was the same for Monsieur Framboise's pantry. Nothing – except the Nibby's, one very stale baguette and the chocolate pot!

'Monsieur Framboise!' said Coco scoldingly. 'I knew it!'

The ghost raised his eyebrows. 'What can I say? You were my enemies . . .' he said, adding, 'back then!'

'We found you in the rafters. Maybe we should try there?' suggested Louis.

Coco and Louis scrambled up the ladder (Monsieur Framboise floated) and checked everywhere that was safe to walk, balancing on the rafters as they went. There was nothing up there, either.

And it was the same in the garden and the future breakfast room and the laundry cupboard and the guest bedrooms. When Coco suggested she search Carmichael's room, however, Monsieur Framboise intervened.

'Never!' he said. 'A guest's room is *interdit* . . . erm, off limits – unless you knock for room service and they tell you to come in, their privacy is sacred!'

'But what if there's a card in there?'

'There wouldn't be – I never liked Room 1.'

'What about in the village?' Coco suggested. 'The first card was in the Murder Cave, away from the hotel. Perhaps you left more in other places?'

'Maybe,' said Monsieur Framboise. 'But I am tied to the hotel. I don't think I can leave. If you search in the village, it must be without me. I will wait in the workshop.'

They didn't have any better ideas. And Carmichael was still all over the place with his phone and his notebook, making it difficult to have a conversation anywhere.

So the friends headed outside, with Belle. She had found the first card – maybe she'd be able to find the next one too.

'Find! Find, Belle!' said Coco. Monsieur Framboise had briefed Belle on the job and she certainly looked like she'd understood. Her tail went up, her nose hit the ground and she immediately started sniffing . . .

. . . around the square . . .

. . . down the hill . . .

. . . along the bakery wall and Café de la Poste's terrace. She looked like she'd been waiting to do this her whole life.

'She is going towards the Murder Cave now,' said Louis.

'Maybe he left more than one card there?' said Coco, hopefully . . .

But Belle found nothing.

'Let's see your notes again, Louis,' said Coco, their heads in the shade, their legs dangling over the edge of the Murder Cave in the sun. Belle found a small puddle to drink from.

They scanned the pages.

'Do you think any of what he said could be clues about the places he left the cards?' she said.

'I do not know,' said Louis. 'He sounded a bit *confus* – muddled I think my cousins would say. I mean, what is the "place where the dead go"?'

Coco shrugged. 'A funeral directors'?'

'There is not one in Mont-Lavande.'

Coco stared at the notes again. 'You wrote "FOREVER" too. That's what Framboise said. So where do the dead go . . . *forever*?'

'Heaven . . . the after-life . . . or whatever you call it?' said Louis. 'That is for all eternity.'

'You can't leave a recipe card there,' Coco observed.

'True.'

The friends thought again, then Louis gasped, 'The *cimetière* . . . erm, graveyard? Once you're there, you're certainly not going anywhere else!'

'It's worth a try . . .'

Belle woofed excitedly as she shot off, nose down, tail up, sniffing the graveyard wall.

Coco and Louis started down the central aisle, where old mausoleums looked out over the lavender fields – their stones cracked and their metal grates rusted by time.

Coco thought the church ahead looked like a mini fortress, with its thick stone walls, narrow arched windows and bell tower – which was leaning precariously to one side. An army of cypress trees stood to the rear of it. And beyond those was the old castle tower.

'Cypress trees protect the dead,' said Louis. 'Well, that is what people here believe. It is why we let rosemary grow wild in graveyards too – to ward off evil spirits.' He grabbed a fistful from a bush on the path's edge, and held it under Coco's nose.

It smelt like Carmichael's tomato and rosemary tart

from the night he'd arrived.

'Do people still come to the church?' asked Coco. 'I've never seen anyone. It looks abandoned.'

'Mostly just hikers and cyclists who like architecture,' said Louis. 'Mum says the church is nineteenth-century. And some people come for funerals. There are still some local family vaults.'

'Family vaults?' said Coco. 'Hmmm. Maybe that's what we should be looking for? A Framboise family tomb? He might have left a recipe there.'

They began searching the grave names, squinting at the worn letters under the blazing sun – Gaboriau, Tiffet (like the baker), Cazeault . . . It was quite moving, at times – it made Coco feel connected to the village and the people who had lived and died there. Some of the newer tombs even had photographs of the people who had died. Louis stopped at one showing an elderly lady with eyes just like his. It read EVELYNE MARTIN', and the dates were 1947 to 2011. 'That is my *grand-mère*,' Louis said. 'I never met her, but Maman has told me so much about her that I feel that I know her, a little.'

'She's the one Monsieur Framboise knew?' asked Coco.

'*Oui.*' And Louis kissed his finger then pressed it to the photo.

Then they set off again, Coco keeping one eye on Belle, who was still sniffing the wall and staying in the shade next to it.

'I'm getting hot,' Coco complained after a while. 'We should be in the shade too.'

And that's when Coco saw it – a large tomb in the corner, smothered in raspberry bushes.

'Louis . . . doesn't Framboise mean raspberry?' she said.

'Yes! Of course!' cried Louis.

They carefully moved the prickly, berry-clad branches out of the way, and there, sure enough, was the Framboise tomb – a relief carving of the hotel at the top of the stone. Not a family vault, just a grave for one person:

ISIDORE FRAMBOISE (1951 – 1981)
Tu es parti, mais ta douceur reste

Coco felt a ball in her throat. 'He was only thirty when he died! That sounds old to us, but it isn't. My parents are both forty-two. What does the inscription say?'

'*Gone, but your sweetness remains.*'

If it had felt odd looking at the photo of Monsieur Framboise in the library book, it was nothing compared to now. Here they were, standing next to his grave, knowing that his body – probably a skeleton now – was somewhere underground, next to them, yet also knowing that he was very much still of this earth, floating around the hotel, looking like he had in life (give or take the ectoplasm and eerie body light and occasional mouse running through his feet). Death was supposed to be final, yet Monsieur Framboise was proof that it wasn't.

'Look, that's odd,' said Coco. There was a freshly cut white rose, nestled among the bushes. 'Do you think someone left it here?'

'*Non, non,*' said Louis with a tut. 'It probably blew in from a nearby grave.'

'The recipe has to be here,' said Coco.

So, they began their search, trying (but failing) to avoid the raspberry prickles as they checked every crevice, every nub, every dip of Monsieur Framboise's gravestone. But . . . no recipe card.

'Coco, it cannot be here!' Louis cried, after at least ten minutes. 'Monsieur Framboise hid the cards before he died. He could not have put one on his own grave!'

'Of course!' Coco felt stupid. They'd wasted so much time. 'Oh, this is hopeless. Let's go back to the hotel.'

'A-woo-woo-woof!'

'Wait,' said Louis.

Belle was up on her hind legs, sniffing a little niche in the wall just behind them.

It contained a beautifully carved statue of a lady with long hair, bare shoulders and a perfume bottle at her feet.

'What have you found, Belle?' said Coco, walking over.

'It is a statue of Marie Madeleine,' said Louis. 'She is the patron saint of perfume-makers. With all the lavender and flowers in this region, there are lots of statues of her, because there are so many perfumers. She is said to bring luck.'

'Louis! Her name!' Coco cried. 'MADELEINE! Monsieur Framboise keeps saying it, do you think . . . ?'

The friends immediately started searching around the statue, behind her feet, her face, her hair. Then Belle barked again and pointed her nose at the perfume bottle, where there was a crack in the stone with just space enough for a fingertip or two to squeeze in.

'I can feel something,' Louis said, pulling the something out.

It was a tiny snail shell.

'Wait, there is something else behind it.' And sure enough, this time, out came a little roll of old card!

'Oh, you clever dog!' cried Coco, ruffling Belle's fur. Belle jumped up and licked her nose, before turning to Louis and doing the same. She looked very pleased with herself.

'What does it say?' asked Coco.

'The recipe is called "*Éternité*",' said Louis, reading the flouncy writing. 'It is for milk chocolate rings with lavender flowers sprinkled on top!'

'Well, Madeleine definitely has something to do with

this,' Coco announced. 'The Murder Cave was where Monsieur Framboise used to go with her – I think. He didn't finish his sentence, but that's what it sounded like. We know she helped around the hotel. And now this statue. Let's get back. We need to find Monsieur Framboise and make these chocolates.'

26

Belle waited patiently outside as Coco and Louis sneaked into Louis's house to grab the ingredients for the recipe (chocolate from the cupboard; dried lavender from a pot in the kitchen; the lot hidden in a shopping bag), then they rushed back to the hotel.

They'd hoped to make it inside unseen, but there was Atticus Carmichael pacing around the small patch of garden by the front door.

It felt odd to Coco, sharing her home with a stranger. Even if TV had made him seem familiar, Coco didn't really know him. *I'll have to get used to it*, she thought. *When the hotel opens properly, there will be lots of strangers here all the time.*

'Oh, hello children!' he said cheerily. 'I was just on the phone to the BBC! I'll be writing the pitch soon.'

'Oh, right!' said Coco, not knowing how to answer.

'I made a cake, if you'd like some. It's inside.'

'Thanks,' said Coco.

'Thank you, too. Any new chocs for me to try yet?'

'No,' she said, adding, 'Sorry!'

'And what about that recipe?' he called after her.

'Almost ready,' she lied.

'Well, I can hardly wait.'

Carmichael had only been there a few days, but the more she saw him, the stranger he seemed. The Carmichael on TV was charming and funny, and he was in person, too – most of the time. Sometimes, though, he seemed a bit . . . *pushy*. It was like he'd taken over the whole hotel.

'Quick, let us go down to the cellar while he is outside,' said Louis.

They stepped into the hidden workshop to find Monsieur Framboise fast asleep, resting mid-air on the point of a broom handle. What a strange sight! It was as if the ghost were part of a magician's trick. He was the peculiar, transparent top of a big letter 'T' – his body horizontal and the broom handle vertical, leaning against the work surface.

'Monsieur Framboise?' whispered Coco, gently. 'Wake up.'

Belle sat by the door at the bottom of the stairs to

keep watch again.

'Hmm . . . *Quoi?*' Monsieur Framboise opened his eyes and, '*Oh là là!*' he grumbled, floating himself upright. 'A broom handle this time! How embarrassing! Alive, I sleepwalked. Dead, I sleepfloat. Don't ask me where else I have woken up this week . . . in your fridge . . . in the U-bend . . . under your parents' bed.'

'Under their bed?'

'Yes, your father has very smelly socks.'

And then he saw it. The recipe card on the work surface. And his tone changed from annoyance to wonder.

'You found one! How? Where?'

'In the graveyard. In the statue of Marie Madeleine,' said Coco.

'You clever children.'

'Rrow!'

'And dog,' said Monsieur Framboise, turning to the door. 'Yes, Belle, I mustn't forget you.'

Then he shoved his head into the card. 'Ah, of course,' he said. '*Éternité!* This was a particularly successful confection. Did you bring the ingredients?'

'Yes.'

'Come on then. *Vite!*'

After *Ganache, je t'aime*, making the *Éternités* was easier, as the children knew the secret technique of stirring to the rhythm of their hearts, to fill the chocolate with love.

'*Très bien, très bien!*' said Monsieur Framboise as Coco melted the chocolate in the bain-marie, one hand on her heart, the other stirring in time to its beat. 'That is going to be beautiful *chocolat*!'

Then he told Louis to get some ring-shaped moulds from the pantry, and showed him how to fill them with the chocolate and sprinkle on the dried lavender.

'*Parfait!*'

The chocolates looked very pretty, like little brown-and-purple wreaths.

'I couldn't have done a better job myself,' said Monsieur Framboise, pocketing the recipe.

And the second it disappeared, the same bright white light appeared around him and he entered another trance – just as disturbing as the first.

Ectoplasm tears welled in his eyes as he whispered, '*Non, non!* I don't want to die! It is not my time . . .' Then, he turned to Coco and Louis. 'No help came . . . I lay there . . . dying . . . on the shop floor! No help came!'

'Who didn't help?' said Coco, trying to pull herself together. 'Can you remember who was there?'

'*Non!*' whispered Monsieur Framboise.

Hands trembling, Louis got out his notepad and pen. 'Is there another card?' he said.

'Yes.'

'Do you know where it is?'

Monsieur Framboise looked frightened again for a moment, then with a wobble in his voice, said, 'Look out . . . Madeleine!'

'What do you mean, *Look out, Madeleine*?' said Coco. 'Who is Madeleine? What did she do?'

'I-I can remember no more,' he said. 'I am sorry.' And the white light around him disappeared.

Coco and Louis dared to breathe again.

'Monsieur Framboise?' said Coco, carefully. 'Do you think this Madeleine has something to do with your death?'

'I told you, I DO NOT want to talk about her!' came the very firm reply.

Then, more warmly (after all, it wasn't their fault he'd been killed), he said, 'Let's taste the chocolates.'

So they did. Well, Coco and Louis did. Monsieur Framboise couldn't taste anything any more. 'But your pleasure is my pleasure,' he said, watching their faces light up as they tucked in.

And it was a welcome moment, because what they had just seen and heard had been so horrible.

Plus, the chocolate rings were utterly delicious.

'Little bonbons of joy, *non*?' said Monsieur Framboise with a new-found grin. 'Pops of sweetness offset by tangy lavender. And made with the magic of love.'

Louis had brought something else from home this time too. 'Cardboard and pens.' He drew them out of the bag. 'The chocolates are so pretty, I think we should make a box for them.'

Coco and Monsieur Framboise watched in awe as Louis folded the paper into a punnet just big enough for all the chocolates to sit in.

'We have to make lots of boxes at home – for our lavender oils and jams and honeys and perfumed sachets,' he said, drawing little chocolates and lavender all over the box. He even copied the old hotel logo. It looked very professional.

'I'm impressed,' said Monsieur Framboise. 'You two have done so well today.' Then he yawned. 'But all this horrible remembering is making me tired. I must rest . . . After I have tidied up.'

'Do you think Madeleine was involved in his death somehow?' whispered Louis, as they emerged into the cellar through the wine cupboard.

'I was thinking the same thing,' said Coco. 'What if she killed him? Every time we bring up her name, Monsieur Framboise gets upset and doesn't want to talk about her. And when you asked if there was another card, he said, *Look out . . . Madeleine!*'

'And we know that Madeleine used to help around the

hotel,' said Louis.

'And think about the name of the other place he hid the recipe,' said Coco. 'The Murder Cave. We have "murder", "Madeleine" and "look out". Maybe it's a clue? We really need to find out who she is. She sounds dangerous.'

They reached the door to the lobby and pushed it open.

'Children!' It was Carmichael. They'd practically walked into him.

Coco cursed herself. How could they have been so careless? She swiftly passed the box of chocolates to Louis behind her back and he slipped them into his bag.

'I thought you weren't allowed down there,' Carmichael said, flicking his hair to one side, like Coco had seen him do so often on TV – usually when he was about to eliminate a contestant.

'Well, we're not. But Dad asked us to get this bag for him,' said Coco, trying to sound normal.

Louis held it up. 'Tools!' he said.

Belle growled.

'Belle, quiet.' Coco pulled the key from her pocket and locked the cellar door tightly behind her.

'So, have you written down that recipe for me yet?' Carmichael smiled, one side of his mouth creeping up faster than the other – not at all like his usual charming smile.

'Not since you last asked me, no,' said Coco. The excitement of having him stay was starting to wear off. He really was insistent. 'I haven't had chance to write it out yet,' she continued. 'Me and Louis have been working on a new idea, you see.'

'Oh, good. I knew it.' He flicked his hair again.

'Yes,' said Coco. 'When it's finished, we'll show you. Probably tomorrow morning. With Mum.' Coco knew a half lie was more believable than a whole lie, and they were going to give the chocolates to Mum, anyway, for her video.

'Well, I look forward to seeing it. The BBC is very interested in the show, but if I am to prove there is a strong food element, I really must see your recipes.' Then he winked and sauntered up the stairs towards his room, his steps hardly making a sound.

'Do you think he suspected anything?' said Coco.

'I do not think so. There is no way he can know about Monsieur Framboise and the workshop.'

'What are we going to do?' said Coco.

Things were getting more complicated by the day.

The next morning, breakfast was French toast made with brioche, cooked to perfection by Carmichael.

Then, 'Ta-da!' Coco and Louis brought out the *Eternité* chocolates and their box, and everyone was amazed – Carmichael especially.

'Lavender and milk chocolate, such an interesting mix!' he boomed, back to his usual charming self. 'Ha! And the purple matches today's bowtie,' he added, pointing theatrically at his neck.

'Wow! Just wow!' said Mum.

'What a beautiful box, Louis,' said Dad. 'It looks fantastic.'

Louis blushed.

Then Mum posted a video of Carmichael eating the chocolates, and within minutes a huge department store in Paris sent her a message asking if they could advertise on her Hôtel Framboise web page.

'For thirty thousand euros?' Dad said in disbelief.

'Yes!' Mum squealed with excitement. 'It'll be enough to finish the guest rooms!'

'You're officially an influencer, my darling.' Dad gave her a big hug, before turning to Carmichael to shake his hand. 'This is all thanks to you, Atticus,' he declared.

'Oh no, no,' said Carmichael. 'Not me. Your daughter's and Louis's chocolates! They're just so good.' He popped another one into his mouth. 'Though I really would like to see their recip—'

'Mum, can I go to Louis's house now?' said Coco quickly. She was pleased for her parents – very pleased – and Monsieur Framboise's chocolates were helping a lot, but she could tell Carmichael was about to turn the conversation back to the recipes, and she didn't want to hear it. She and Louis needed to talk.

'So, we've got another card to find,' said Coco, sitting cross-legged by Louis on his bedroom floor, staring at his notes. Belle had stayed behind at the hotel for her nap. 'But this Madeleine person seems to be the key to it all, so I think we should try to find out who she is first.'

'Agreed. Presuming she is still alive,' said Louis. 'And still lives round here.'

'But if she really is the murderer, we'll need to be very careful.' Coco gulped. 'I wonder why Monsieur Framboise won't tell us who she is.'

'Maybe he cannot. He cannot remember who killed him, after all.'

'Hmmm. Another reason it could be her.'

They thought for a moment.

'Your mum and dad sell lavender to lots of people, don't they?' said Coco.

'*Oui.*'

'They might have a Madeleine as a client. I think we should ask them. We can tell them you're researching names for your summer holiday homework or something.'

Louis's dad was in the home office, so they tried there first.

'Madeleine?' he said, once they'd told him about the supposed homework. '*Désolé. Non.* I don't know anybody with that name. But ask Maman, she's in the oil distillery.'

So, soon they were on their bikes, cycling from Louis's house in the village to the Ferme Martin at the bottom of the hill. The distillery room lay at the end of a corridor through some double doors, and smelt so strongly of lavender, Coco thought it was like standing in a perfume bottle.

'There could be a Madeleine among our clients,' said Louis's mum popping her head out from behind a copper tank. 'But I can't think of any I know personally. But you know who might be able to help? Madame Tiffet,' she suggested. 'She knows most people around here.'

So off they went, puffing their way back up the hill to the bakery.

But Madame Tiffet didn't know a Madeleine either.

'That only leaves Monsieur Dubois at the cafe,' said Louis.

It was hot (and their legs were tired from pedalling up the hill), so the friends stopped for a quick drink – apple juice for Coco and a bright green drink called *diabolo menthe* (mint syrup with lemonade) for Louis, which – 'Urgh!' – Coco thought tasted like fizzy toothpaste.

'*Non, désolé,*' said Monsieur Dubois, carrying a tray of empty bottles past the post office counter to the old wooden bar. '*Je ne connais pas de Madeleine.*' Then Louis followed him to the bar and exchanged a few more words.

'Let me guess,' said Coco, as Louis sat back down. 'He doesn't know a Madeleine?'

Louis shook his head. 'No. And I asked him if he ever sees the names on the letters. He does not. He said he just sells stamps and receives the post bags. It is a *facteur* . . . erm . . . a *post worker*, who delivers the mail from a van.'

'Who *is* the post worker?'

'No idea,' said Louis. 'The old one retired. Mum has been complaining about it. She liked him.'

'Oh, this is impossible,' said Coco. 'Maybe we should go back to searching for the card?'

'Not yet,' said Louis. 'I have an idea. Look, there is a post bag by the counter. We could look through it. See if we can find a letter for a Madeleine in it. The envelope will have her *adresse* on it, then we can check her out.'

'That's brilliant. OK. You talk to Monsieur Dubois and distract him, while I see what I can find.'

Louis slunk over to where Monsieur Dubois was now tidying some glasses, and started asking questions – how many villages does the post office cover? ('Three.') How hot was it going to be today? ('Very. Probably. It's summer.') Was it difficult running both a cafe and a post office in the same building? ('Oh yes, very tiring!') It was a bit awkward, because Monsieur Dubois kept giving short answers and looked like he wanted to get on with his work without stopping to talk.

Coco crept the other way, to the post bag, opened it and quickly riffled through the letters. And there, suddenly, were not one but two Madeleines.

She gave Louis a sneaky thumbs-up and he came back over as Monsieur Dubois went into the kitchen.

'Look – there's a Madeleine Reynaud in Bellevue, the same village as the library. And a Madeleine Daumont in . . . where does that say?'

'Ville-Verte.'

'Where's that?'

'The next village after Bellevue. We can bike to both.'

Coco immediately took the letters and slipped them under her T-shirt.

'What are you doing?' Louis looked round at the kitchen door – thankfully Monsieur Dubois hadn't come back through yet.

'If Madeleine is still alive, she'll probably be old by now,' said Coco. 'So, we're going to deliver these by hand.' She tapped her T-shirt. 'Or rather you are – I can't speak French, remember. We'll say they accidentally got posted through our door so, as we were passing through, we thought we'd deliver them. This way, we get to see if one of the Madeleines fits the age at least.'

'What if she is the murderer?'

'We'll just have to be very careful.'

The bike ride to Bellevue seemed to go faster than the first time – probably because Coco wasn't taking in the sights like before and because Louis wasn't stopping in the woods to draw deadly nightshade (though he did notice the nightshade had finished flowering and now had dark, shiny berries).

'The address is 21 rue du Château,' said Louis as they huffed up the steep slope to Bellevue's main square. 'That is just over here.'

They found the house and rang the bell.

Coco scuffed the sole of her trainers on the kerb as they waited, trying not to think about what a murderous Madeleine might do to them. It was one thing saying 'We'll be careful!', but quite another standing in front of a door, about to meet her.

But no one came. For a second, Coco didn't know which was worse. The annoyance of not finding her or the relief of not having to face a potential killer.

They were just about to go when a young woman with a Jack Russell terrier stopped at the door.

'*Bonjour!*' said Louis. They spoke for a moment, then the woman smiled, and Louis gave her the letter before turning away with a disappointed look.

'Wrong Madeleine. Too young!' he said, getting back on his bike.

So off they went, towards the village of Ville-Verte.

And this time, they had to go on a road with traffic.

It was a first for Coco, and it felt very strange cycling on the right-hand side of the road. Not at all the same as when Mum and Dad drove with her in the car.

Soon, much to her relief, they arrived at a pretty house set into the rock on the edge of Ville-Verte. 'Why *do* you drive on the left in Britain, anyway?' Louis asked, as they knocked on the door.

'Dad told me once it was because of highwaymen – you know, old road bandits. You had to drive your horse-drawn carriage on the left so that your sword arm was free to fight on the right.'

'What if you were left-handed?'

'Then you got robbed, I guess.'

They both laughed, but stopped abruptly when an

elderly lady answered the door.

Coco's heart sped up. Was this it? Was this their murderer?

Louis stepped forward, trying not to panic. But after exchanging only a few words, he'd handed the lady the letter and was heading back to his bike.

'Well?' said Coco.

'That was the mother of Madeleine Daumont, which means Madeleine Daumont is also too young to be our Madeleine.'

'We'll never find her at this rate!' Coco complained.

Then, back at the hotel, things got worse.

There in the lobby were Dad and Carmichael, preparing to carry dozens of boxes into the wine cellar.

Coco half expected to find Monsieur Framboise whooshing around in a tizzy, but he must still have been resting because he wasn't there.

'W-what are you doing?' Coco asked, trying to sound casual. The cellar door was wide open.

'Well, this is France,' said Carmichael, one side of his smile creeping further up his cheek again. 'So, I thought it was about time the hotel had some decent wine in the cellar. Well, wine, full stop!' he said, winking at Dad.

'Atticus has kindly bought us three hundred bottles!' said Dad. 'All from local vineyards. I still can't believe it!'

'Oh, it's nothing, honestly. I want to thank you for

opening the hotel to me so thoroughly. Plus, I'm making good progress with the BBC.' He rested a box on the top step to the cellar and panted. 'This wine will boost the food and drink element of the pitch, then you just need to do a bit of DIY down here, to get it shipshape for the cameras, eh Burt?'

'Absolutely!'

Coco and Louis just stared at each other, panic rising in both their chests. This was terrible. If Dad renovated the wine cellar, they'd discover Monsieur Framboise's secret workshop.

'Erm . . . what sort of DIY?' Coco asked.

'Rip out that old wine cupboard for a start,' said Carmichael. 'Get some lovely modern shelves up, and perhaps some special fridges for the white wines.'

Coco wanted to scream.

'W-when do you plan to start?' she stuttered.

'Oh, as soon as possible!' said Carmichael.

'Well, in the next few days,' Dad corrected. 'We need to buy the shelving first. We'd better get back to it, this lot won't shift itself.'

Once Dad and Carmichael had gone into the cellar, Coco turned to Louis. 'Do you think Carmichael suspects something?' she whispered. 'I mean, he saw us coming out of there the other day.'

'I still do not think so,' Louis replied. 'Why would he?

He does not know anything about Monsieur Framboise. Or the recipe cards. Or the workshop. And we hid the chocolates. But I think we should warn Monsieur Framboise about it.'

'No,' said Coco. 'Well, not yet. We need him to concentrate on how he died. Let's try and work out who killed him first. If it brings him peace, he might – you know – move on, then maybe we won't have to worry about telling him about the cellar renovations, because he won't be here any more.'

And the second she said it, she felt sad. For in that moment, she understood that she'd begun to like Monsieur Framboise. A lot. She'd miss him when he was gone.

'Come on,' said Coco with a sigh. 'Let's go to my room.'

'Oh, and children!' Carmichael suddenly emerged from the cellar steps. 'That's two recipes you must show me now. I was just telling your father, Coco, what a huge difference they'll make to my offerings to the BBC.'

There was something about the way he said it that set Coco on edge.

'Perhaps you could write them out for Atticus tomorrow, sweetheart?' Dad said, coming up behind the chef. 'He's been so good to us; it's the least we could do.'

'OK,' Coco squeaked.

'Thank you,' said Carmichael. 'You and Louis are so talented. The world needs to know.'

The next morning, Coco awoke to the sound of voices outside.

She looked through her window, and there was Carmichael, in the square, with Mum, Dad, Belle and about thirty other people!

What on earth was going on? Mont-Lavande was usually very sleepy. She dressed quickly and rushed down.

There were people taking selfies with Carmichael in front of the 'Chocolatier' sign. Mum and Dad were chatting to a group of cyclists about the renovations. Belle was greeting everyone with a waggy tail, and occasionally lying on her back for a tickle. Even Madame Auguste was there.

'It is you!' she cried, pointing at Carmichael.

'Indeed, it is!' he answered, strolling over with a smile to shake her hand, and trying not to look surprised when she turned her back and hobbled back towards her house.

'What is happening?' Louis said, tapping Coco on the shoulder.

'Beats me,' said Coco. Just then, a girl about their age came over, waving her phone.

'Can . . . I . . . selfie?' she said in broken English.

'Erm, yes . . .' This was weird. 'Why?'

The girl leant in and took the photo.

'Because . . . *chocolats*!' She'd attempted to keep speaking in English, but had got so shy that she carried on in French.

Coco knew the feeling.

'Her name is Romy,' said Louis, once she'd left. 'She is from my school. The year above, I think. She said she has seen all the videos your mum made about the hotel and the chocolates, and that people are here because Carmichael posted a video saying he would give free chocolate to anyone who came here this morning!'

'What?' Coco looked over and, sure enough, there was a table set up in the square with a tray of chocolates.

She and Louis rushed over.

'What's going on?' Coco asked her parents, who were posing for a photo in front of the 'Chocolatier' sign. 'Did you know about this?'

'No!' said Mum. 'But isn't it wonderful? Atticus wanted to surprise us.'

'To help drum up more attention,' said Dad. 'And it's worked! I could get used to this.'

Coco and Louis walked over to the tray, where pretty little chocolate squares sprinkled with purple petals sat in neat rows.

'He's put lavender on them, like our rings,' said Coco.

They popped one into their mouths and . . .

'Well?' said Carmichael, striding over with his TV smile on his face.

'Nice and sweet,' said Louis. The chocolate had ganache in the middle, too.

'Yes, lovely,' said Coco, thinking, *Lavender, ganache – it's like a mix of everything we've made so far.*

But they weren't as good as the ones they'd made with Monsieur Framboise, and it was clear that Carmichael knew it too.

'Thank you!' he said. 'Not your recipe, of course. But one does what one can, when one hasn't received what one has been promised.' He stared at them for an uncomfortably long amount of time, before turning back to an adoring fan.

'Let us go,' said Louis. 'To my house. We need to work out what to do next.'

Coco couldn't wait to get away. She checked with Mum and Dad, then told Belle to come with them. But Belle only got as far as Madame Auguste's letterbox, where she stopped dead and wouldn't stop sniffing.

'Belle, come!' called Coco. 'We're going to Louis's place.'

But the dog wouldn't budge.

'Naughty, Belle!' Coco pulled on Belle's collar. And that's when she saw it. The name on the letterbox: *Madame M. Auguste*. She'd noticed it the day she'd gone looking for Louis's house, but had totally forgotten about it.

M. Auguste! No! It couldn't be . . . ?

'Louis?' she called. 'Do you think Madame Auguste could be Madeleine?'

'No way,' Louis declared. 'I have lived here all my life. I would know if she was called Madeleine. Mum and Dad too, and everyone else in the village.'

'But she keeps herself to herself,' said Coco.

'Yes, but—'

'What does the "M" stand for, then?' said Coco.

Louis thought for a second. 'Marguerite . . . Marie . . .'

Coco raised her eyebrows.

'OK, I do not know, but there is a way we can find out. It is Wednesday. She will go shopping soon – for hours. We can watch for her to leave from my house, then check her letterbox for anything with her name on.'

It didn't take long. Just time enough for a quick croissant (and a raw carrot for Belle) at Louis's, then there was Madame Auguste, hobbling towards her little blue car, walking stick and shopping bags in tow. And then she was gone.

'Quick!'

Grabbing a metal coat hanger from the closet in Louis's hall, they went to the old lady's letterbox.

Coco scanned the square. Mum, Dad and Carmichael were nowhere to be seen, but there were still a few hangers-on taking selfies – Romy included.

'Coast clear!' Coco said, once she was sure no one was looking.

In went the coat hanger, Louis bending it gently through the slit. Out came . . . an old-fashioned clothes catalogue on its hook.

'Let me see!' said Coco, grabbing the catalogue. And there it was. In neat black print: *Madeleine Auguste!*

The friends just stared.

'I cannot believe it,' said Louis. 'She has been under our noses all this time!'

'She has to be the Madeleine we're looking for,' said Coco. 'She hates other people, lives close to the crime scene, hardly leaves the house . . . If anyone's a murderer around here, it's her.'

'But what are we going to do? We cannot talk to her,' said Louis. 'If she did kill Monsieur Framboise, letting her know that *we* know could be dangerous. We might be next.'

'You're right,' said Coco. 'That's why we're going to break into her house!'

'BREAK IN!' Louis looked horrified. 'Oh, *non, non, non*! We will get into trouble.'

'Yes, but trouble's better than being killed,' said Coco. She sounded brave, but her innards were mush. 'Maybe we'll find something linked to Monsieur Framboise or the hotel in there. Murderers always keep mementoes from their crimes – well, on TV they do.'

'I don't know . . .' said Louis.

'Come on, you said she'd be gone for hours,' Coco pleaded. She was just as scared as Louis. Terrified even. But they had to do this. For Monsieur Framboise. For her parents and the hotel. 'Belle can keep watch by the door. We'll be in and out before you know it.'

Louis didn't look happy, but he followed her through the garden to the back door.

Belle settled down outside. It was as if she knew what to do.

Then Coco found a metal trowel on the floor.

'What is that for?'

'To break the window.' She knew it was wrong, but how else would they get in?

Louis tried the door handle.

'Erm, Coco . . . it is not locked!'

'Oh!' Coco looked surprised.

'*Bah*, people round here often leave their doors open – we do not get much crime.'

'Says the boy about to step into a murderer's home!'

Louis gulped in reply.

Madame Auguste's house was like a museum. Everything was neat and old, and a shade of orange or brown – from the shaggy rug and floor tiles in the dining room, to the settee and matching wallpaper in the sitting area and hall. The only thing white was the netting on the windows. The house looked frozen in time.

Coco and Louis tiptoed through the sitting area, feeling sick with nerves.

'Where would a murderer put their keepsakes?' whispered Coco.

'Maman puts ours in our *buffet* . . . sideboard,' said Louis, adding, 'but she is not a murderer!'

'There's a sideboard there.' Coco walked over and

opened the drawers and cupboards. 'Just old cutlery and plates in here.'

Then Louis spotted a glass-fronted cabinet, so they tried it. 'Locked.' He still looked terrified.

Coco peered in. 'It's OK. I think there's just a bunch of old knick-knacks.'

They kept on going, opening drawers and cupboards and even the fridge.

'I do not think there is anything else downstairs,' said Louis. 'Let us try upstairs.'

They crept up the staircase to the bedroom – all blue and white with frills. A vase of white roses sat on the bedside table and a huge wooden trunk sat in the corner.

'I bet there's something in there,' said Coco, pointing at the trunk. 'If I was a murderer, it's where I'd put stuff. Here, help me open it.'

Louis came over and together they heaved the lid open to reveal . . .

'A pile of old tablecloths?' said Coco, disappointed.

'No. Not just old tablecloths, Coco.' Louis was pointing at the corners. 'There are embroidered letters, look: "H" and "F".'

'Hôtel Framboise.' Coco leant closer. 'I wonder if there's anything undernea—'

She didn't need to finish, because Louis had already lifted them up to reveal: 'Monsieur Framboise!'

Well, not the real Monsieur Framboise (obviously). But his photo, on top of a pile of old newspaper cuttings.

'I knew it,' said Coco. 'Mementoes!' Her hands were shaking. This was huge. 'What do the clippings say?' She handed Louis a bunch of the newspapers.

'Hmmm . . . this one talks about the chocolate shop opening in 1980. This mentions the death of Monsieur Framboise, in 1981. It is the same as the one we saw in the library. And this looks like a hotel breakfast menu.'

The friends just stared at each other as the enormity of what they had discovered sank in.

'I think we should get out of here,' said Louis. 'We have found what we need to know.'

But at that moment Belle's barking filled the staircase.

'Get out, or I'll call the police!' There was Madeleine Auguste in the doorway, back early, and brandishing her walking stick.

Belle rushed into the bedroom growling, standing between Madame Auguste and Coco.

'G-go ahead! Call them!' Coco cried. 'We know you did it!'

'Did what?'

'Killed Monsieur Isidore Framboise, hotelier and master chocolatier!'

The sound of the name surprised Madame Auguste so much that, for a moment, she swooned and had to steady herself on her stick.

'I-I didn't kill Isidore,' she stuttered. 'I loved him!' She looked confused and ready to cry. 'We were supposed to be married!'

Coco felt a ball of panic fill her stomach.

'Then he di—' She couldn't finish. She put a hand to her chest, overcome with emotion. 'I imagine him all the time. I see his face looking out of the hotel window every night.'

And in that second, Coco realized she and Louis had made a terrible mistake.

'It's not your imagination,' Coco said, hoping that telling the truth might somehow make the situation better. 'He's a ghost.'

'How dare you!' snapped Madame Auguste. 'First you break in, then you tease me. Your parents will hear about this.'

'No, that's n-not what I meant,' Coco stuttered. Oh, my goodness! She felt squirmy inside. Looking at Madame Auguste now, it seemed ridiculous to have ever thought she was a murderer. She looked frail. And damaged. Just a poor lady with a broken heart. These weren't murderous mementoes – they were memories.

And they'd just broken into her house!

'I think you children should leave, now,' Madame Auguste whispered.

Coco had never wanted to run away faster, but Louis held her back.

'Madame Auguste, we are sorry,' he said, then continued in French, softly. Coco had no idea what he was saying, but little by little, Madame Auguste's face relaxed and her grip on her walking stick loosened. And then, much to Coco's surprise, she limped over to her bed and sat down.

'A ghost, you say?' she said. 'Poor Isidore! When I saw him at the window, I didn't dare believe it was real. My love, alone for so long in that empty building! I should have been there for him, but I was so sad, I couldn't bring myself to set foot in the hotel.'

Belle placed her head on Madame Auguste's knee.

'Madame Auguste,' said Coco, carefully. 'I am so sorry we broke in, and that we've made you sad, but . . .' It was now or never. She told her all about the haunting, about how they'd found the first recipe card – *Ganache, je t'aime* – by accident in the Murder Cave.

How the recipe had helped Monsieur Framboise remember he was murdered.

That there were other cards.

That his ramblings had given them just enough clues to find the second one, *Éternité*.

How Monsieur Framboise wanted to be at peace, but couldn't leave because he had unfinished business:

discovering who killed him.

And that now they were looking for a third card to see if that would help him remember.

'Isidore and his recipe cards,' said Madame Auguste, with a sad chuckle. 'They were his most precious belongings. He put them into a book, which he hid in a secret place. Even I didn't know where that was. Then every year, on Valentine's Day, he'd leave three recipes for me to find. I never found the ones you have discovered, because that is the day he died.'

Madame Auguste stared sadly into space for a moment.

'You found the *Ganache, je t'aime* recipe in the Murder Cave because that is where we would go to talk, to be alone. It was where he told me he loved me. The graveyard card – *Éternité* – was because that was where he asked me to marry him. Some people think graveyards are frightening, but I think they are romantic. Isidore and I loved each other so much, we planned to be together in life and in death.'

'Madame Auguste,' Coco dared to ask, 'do you know what, "Look out . . . Madeleine" might mean? It was the last clue.'

Madame Auguste thought for a second, then nodded solemnly.

'The tower!'

The tower?

'It is where we first kissed. We weren't supposed to climb. It was dangerous, but Isidore said the views were the best in the world, so we went up to look out. We carved our initials.'

Coco felt embarrassed. *Look out . . . Madeleine* hadn't meant she was dangerous at all. It had meant 'look out over the valley, Madeleine, you can see for miles'.

Then it was Louis's turn to ask a question. 'Do you know anything about the day Monsieur Framboise died?'

Madame Auguste took a tissue from her bedside table and blew her nose. 'A little,' she said. 'He'd had a friend here, Nicolas Nibbsworth. Everyone called him Nibby. He was English. His family had a chocolate factory in London.'

Coco looked at Louis, wide-eyed. 'Nibby's chocolates!' she said, remembering not just the Nibby's flying around her room, but how the company had liked Mum's first chocolate post. Coco couldn't believe it.

'Isidore and Nibby studied cooking in Paris together,' Madame Auguste continued. 'They became friends. Nibby was younger than Isidore by ten years, but was so talented. A prodigy. They inspired each other. Nibby won many prizes, but Isidore was the chocolate master. He won the most prestigious chocolate-making prize there is, the Chocolatier's Cup. It was the only trophy Nibby never got, and he wanted to learn from Isidore, to take his family factory to another level. Come, I will show you.'

The children and Belle followed Madame Auguste downstairs to the sitting area. She headed straight for the knick-knack cabinet they'd tried earlier and unlocked it, then reached to the back and took out a gleaming, gold-coloured cup. It read *1980 Winner: Isidore Framboise*. She placed it on the dining table.

'It's very beautiful,' said Coco.

'There was prize money, too. He used it to build the chocolate shop. He had inherited the hotel from his uncle, Étienne Gaboriau, a few years before...'

Gaboriau! thought Coco. *That's the name we saw in the graveyard.*

'... Nibby was there the day Isidore died,' Madame Auguste continued, her hands shaking a little. 'The police said Isidore accidentally ate poison, and Nibby was the one who found him. But I always wondered...'

'Wondered what?' said Coco.

'Whether he'd had something to do with his death. Nibby was always changeable – charming one minute, moody the next, and always so jealous of Isidore's chocolates. Isidore even caught him trying to steal a recipe card one day. He was so disappointed. Their friendship was never the same after that. Isidore hid his book in a new secret place, and built a new workshop – in the old castle *oubliettes* below the wine cellar. He did it all himself. And never told anyone where the workshop was. Except me, *bien sûr*. And you now too.

'Then, I never saw Nibby again, until . . . Oh, *je ne sais pas*. That man staying at the hotel . . .'

'Carmichael?'

'*Oui*. He looks like Nibby – or how I imagine Nibby would look decades later. That's why I've been watching.'

'You might have recognized him from TV,' said Coco. 'He's very famous.'

'I do not watch TV,' Madame Auguste said. 'And today, when I saw him with the chocolates . . . I think it's him!'

Coco's brain felt ready to explode. That's why Madame Auguste had said, 'It is you!' She wasn't a fan of Carmichael's – she'd recognized him.

'C-Coco?' said Louis, positively trembling now. 'Monsieur Framboise was murdered and Madame Auguste thinks Nibby was involved. If Nibby murdered him, and Nibby is Carmichael, then . . .'

'We have a murderer in our house! Yes, I know.' Coco felt like she'd been thumped in the stomach. 'But not everything lines up,' she said. 'If Carmichael was Nibby, it means he's been here before. And yet Carmichael doesn't seem like he knows the hotel. Plus, he's really helping

Mum and Dad. Madame Auguste, do you think Carmichael recognized *you*?'

'I don't know! I thought so for a moment, but . . .'

'Thank you! Thank you so much,' cried Coco, leaping to her feet and pulling Louis towards the door. 'I'm so sorry we broke in. But we've really got to go. Come, Belle!'

'Coco. Where are we going?' cried Louis, racing after her and Belle.

'The tower,' Coco shouted back. 'To find the card.' She stopped to catch her breath. 'We can't go around accusing a world-famous TV chef of being a murderer without more evidence.' After Madame Auguste, she'd learnt her lesson. 'We need to jog Monsieur Framboise's memory. Make the chocolate. See if he remembers who did it.'

They rushed across the village, around the back of the church to the tower.

Belle gave an indignant bark as Coco tied her lead to a tree.

'It's not for dogs,' Coco cooed. 'You keep watch down here.'

Belle sniffed disapprovingly, but settled in the shade.

'How are *we* going to get up there?' Coco cried. The ancient building was tall, with cracks in the walls. It looked very dangerous.

Louis walked over to an old wooden door at the tower's base. It had a big keyhole and a rusty padlock. 'I think there is a staircase behind here,' he said, peering through the keyhole. 'But it is lock—'

Coco had already grabbed a stone and, with all her might, slammed it against the padlock.

CLICK!

It fell off.

'Wow!' said Louis. 'Remind me not to annoy you when you are angry.'

Coco smiled and pushed open the door, before starting up the spiral staircase beyond. Louis followed closely behind.

The higher they climbed, the more the tower seemed to sway.

After forty or so steps, Louis said, 'This is horrible!'

'Uh-huh!' Coco didn't dare talk. She was too nervous, and needed to concentrate on keeping her footing. An arrow slot to her left showed her they now were higher than the village rooftops. If the tower broke or they fell, they were dead!

And yet they climbed. They had to. They had to find

the card.

The staircase suddenly grew more uneven.

Louis slipped. 'ARGH!'

He grabbed Coco's ankle, but she slipped too, and for a second they slid, which made the tower tremble.

'Try to stay still!' Coco cried, her fingers digging into the grooves between the stones for grip.

Louis hit his shin on a step, but managed to regain his balance.

'That was close!' he cried. 'We should go back down. It is too dangerous.' He looked pale and shaken.

Coco felt the same. But then she thought of Carmichael at home with her parents. If he *was* a murderer . . .

'No,' she said. 'We need the card.'

And so slowly, carefully, their arms and legs shaking, they continued their climb.

The roof of the tower was tiny, no more than three feet wide, with walls that reached no higher than their hips. Coco and Louis clung on to the wall.

Madame Auguste had been right: climbing the watchtower was dangerous – dizzyingly so – but the views were breathtaking. Endless patchworks of purple, yellow and green, rolling into snow-capped mountains one way and the azure sea the other. And for a moment, they just stood there, mesmerized. Coco could see why Monsieur Framboise had brought Madeleine up here.

'Look for any holes the card could be tucked in,' she said, snapping them out of it. They didn't have much time.

'It is a ruin. There are many holes,' Louis replied.

Coco's eyes scanned the wall. She thrust her fingertips into a few grooves but there was nothing big enough for a recipe card. Then she saw it – a heart shape carved into a little stone at the base of the wall, just behind Louis.

'There's an engraving down there.' She pointed past his feet. 'Do you think you can twist?'

'I think so,' said Louis, moving slowly so as not to lose his balance. 'I can see an "I" and "M" in it – Isidore and Madeleine. I will feel around.'

Coco didn't dare move; she just watched as Louis dug his nails into every nearby nook, and then, sure enough . . .

'I can feel something.' He smiled, scraping at a gap with his finger until out came a tight roll of card! He unrolled it carefully. 'It is called *Baiser au chocolat* – Chocolate Kiss!' he said triumphantly.

'Makes sense,' said Coco. 'This is where they had their first kiss. What do we need?'

'Milk chocolate and raspberry jam.'

'We have those at home,' said Coco, pocketing the recipe. She stared back at the uneven steps. 'If we survive the climb down!'

32

'Never again!' said Louis as they exited the tower.

Coco couldn't have agreed more. Her legs were still trembling, and she couldn't tell whether it was worry about Carmichael or terror from the tower. Or both.

'A-WOO-WOO-WOO!' Belle scolded them for being so reckless.

But there was no time for a breather.

They needed to get back to Monsieur Framboise.

They arrived in the front garden to find Mum and Dad in the shade, sanding a shelf.

'Is Carmichael here?' Coco asked coolly, hiding the thoughts swirling round her brain.

Did Carmichael do it?

Will Monsieur Framboise remember?

What will we do if either answer is yes?

'No. He's gone out,' said Mum, hardly looking up. 'Something about a walk in the woods.'

Good! She didn't want him around her parents right now.

They grabbed the ingredients from the kitchen, then headed straight for the cellar door, locking it quietly behind them.

'Let's not tell Monsieur Framboise about the Nibby–Carmichael thing yet,' said Coco as they pulled the lever in the wine cupboard. 'Let's see what he remembers first.'

Monsieur Framboise was awake this time and, despite his big grin, seemed nervous to see them. Coco wasn't surprised.

She and Louis were nervous too – about Carmichael, obviously. They had no idea what they'd do if he *was* the murderer. But also because in that moment, it was clear to them that this might be the last time they'd all be together. If Monsieur Framboise remembered his murder now, he'd move on forever. And they'd never see each other again.

Coco suddenly wished she could hug him.

'*Alors*, did you find it?' said Monsieur Framboise, trying to be cheerful.

Coco pulled the recipe card from her pocket and laid it on the work surface.

Belle trotted over to her usual position by the door.

Monsieur Framboise took a deep breath. 'OK. *On y va!*' He thrust his face into the card, then popped back up, saying, 'Ah, my *Baiser au chocolat*! Of course. It was my favourite. *Petits* kisses of sweet *chocolat* and even sweeter raspberry jam. Where was it?'

'At the top of the tower,' said Louis.

'The tower? Whatever was I thinking? It is a deathtrap!'

'We noticed,' said Coco. She gave Louis an anxious glance. 'It was Madeleine who said it might be there,' she said, half expecting the ghost to get angry.

'Madeleine? You found her?' he said, looking suddenly concerned. 'How is she? Does she look well? Did she mention me?'

'She talked about you a lot,' said Coco. 'I don't think she ever got over your death.'

'Really?' he whimpered. He seemed surprised.

'She still lives on the square,' said Louis.

'I know,' said Monsieur Framboise solemnly. 'Why do you think I stare out of the windows? It is not to watch the world. It is in the hope of seeing her!'

'But if you remembered her, why didn't you tell us?' asked Coco, confused.

'B-because . . .' Monsieur Framboise stuttered, looking ready to cry. 'It was too painful. I loved her. I still love her. I couldn't bear to talk about her. I thought she had forgotten me. I cannot leave and she never once came back to the hotel.'

'She didn't know you were a ghost,' replied Coco, thinking back to what Madame Auguste had said. 'She told us she misses *you* so much that it was too painful for her to step foot in the hotel.'

Monsieur Framboise flickered in and out of focus for a second. And Coco wondered if it was the equivalent of a ghostly swoon. How sad their story was: two people in love – one a ghost, the other alive – both pining for each other on opposite sides of the square, yet never communicating. So many years apart. Emotions were funny things, she thought. She felt her heart would burst.

The ghost was lost in thought after that, preparing the bain-marie in silence and not even guessing the percentage of cocoa in the chocolate – which was quite unlike him. He didn't even talk when Louis filled the oval moulds with too much jam, and only signalled with his hand when Coco poured too little chocolate over the top to seal them. Coco wondered if it was because he realized that if he did move on now, he might never see Madeleine again either.

Then before they knew it, the chocolates were ready.

'Children,' said Monsieur Framboise, 'any second now, I will go into my trance.' He pocketed the recipe. 'So I want to say thank y—'

Too late. The bright halo of light had surrounded Monsieur Framboise.

'It is starting,' Louis whispered.

'Chocolate-coated blueberries! *Fantastique*,' said Monsieur Framboise, quite cheerfully. 'What did you say they were called, again? Blueberry Delights?' He placed the imaginary chocolates into his mouth. Then . . .

'Oh, Nibby! Well done. These are delicious.'

'Nibby!' Coco whispered to Louis.

Then Monsieur Framboise dropped to his knees, clutching his throat. 'Not blueberries,' he cried. 'Deadly nightshade!'

He stared straight ahead, as if performing a macabre one-man show. 'He was my friend,' he howled. 'But he left me there . . . dying . . . while he searched for . . .'

'Searched for what?' said Coco.

'My recipe book!'

Recipes!

Coco felt in a daze. This wasn't real. It couldn't be!

'Monsieur Framboise?' said Louis. 'Can you remember what Nibby looked like?'

'*Oui* . . . of course. Like our paying guest. Carmichael!'

And the second he said it, the light went away and he came to.

But he didn't disappear!

Which was odd, as he'd finally remembered how

he'd died.

But there was no time to dwell on that.

'Carmichael *is* the murderer!' Coco cried. *Madame Auguste was right.* 'Louis! We've been living with a murderer. A MURDERER! We're in danger!'

'Madame Auguste, too,' said Louis. 'Think about it – he knows we have the recipes, but he does not know we know anything else. But Madame Auguste . . . she recognized him as Nibby this morning. If he recognized her, he will know she could link him to the death of Monsieur Framboise.'

'Not my Madeleine!' whimpered the ghost.

'Monsieur Framboise, stay here so we can find you,' Coco ordered. 'We're going to warn everyone.'

33

'Pull the other one,' said Mum. 'A ghost helped you make the chocolates in a secret workshop below the cellar, which you get to through the wine cupboard, which is actually a door?'

'Carmichael is really called Nicolas Nibbsworth, and owns the Nibby's chocolate empire?' said Dad. 'And we're in danger of him murdering us and Madame Auguste?'

Mum and Dad had been in the kitchen on a tea break when Coco and Louis had found them. Now, they were laughing so hard their chairs squeaked.

'But it *is* true!' Coco and Louis cried together.

Coco had told them everything about Monsieur Framboise, the cards, talking to Madame Auguste (she left out the breaking-in part), Carmichael really being

Nibby, the deadly nightshade . . . but they'd not believed a word.

'I know it sounds far-fetched . . .'

'That's the least I'd say,' said Mum. 'Ghosts don't exist, for a start.'

'And why would a famous TV chef want to murder us when he's helping us get a TV show with the BBC?' said Dad.

'Because all he really wants are Monsieur Framboise's recipes! That's why he's been asking for them all the time. He'll kill us for them, and for knowing he's killed before!'

'Don't be so ridiculous!' said Mum. 'Who'd murder for something as insignificant as a recipe?'

'I've heard enough!' said Dad.

Coco could tell her parents were getting impatient, but she had to get through to them.

'Mum, Dad! You've got to listen to me,' she cried. 'I know this sounds impossible, but you have to trust us! WE ARE IN DANGER! You need to get out of the hotel NOW and call the police! Go to Louis's house. Tell his parents what's going on. Please! We're going to warn Madame Auguste.'

Without waiting for an answer, she, Louis and Belle dashed outside.

As they raced across the square, Coco could hear her parents' voices behind her.

'Enough of this nonsense, Coco Bean!' cried Mum. 'We will not have you dragging our elderly neighbour into this.'

'You will apologize to her, right away,' cried Dad. 'And you should too, Louis! I can't believe— Huh? What's going on here?'

As they all arrived at Madame Auguste's front door, they found it was ajar, and a terrible gurgling noise was coming from inside.

'GRRR!' growled Belle.

'I hope we're not too late!' Coco whispered to Louis. She was trembling all over.

'Madame Auguste!' called Mum, sensing something was off. '*Vous êtes là?*'

There was no reply.

Coco dared to push open the door.

Madame Auguste's walking stick was lying on the floor.

'She must have had a fall,' said Mum. 'Quick!'

They piled in. But Madame Auguste hadn't had a fall, though she was on the ground. She'd been attacked.

And there, standing over her pale, frail body was her attacker still, watching PURPLE CHOCOLATE-COATED BERRIES tumble from her mouth . . .

'ATTICUS?' Mum screamed.

'Guilty as charged! Again.' Carmichael turned around

with a mad smile. 'Anyone for a Blueberry Delight?'

Belle immediately jumped on him, snarling, biting at his trouser leg. He managed to kick her away, before dashing through to the back of the house and escaping out the garden door.

'AAAAARRGH!' Mum shrieked. 'Call an ambulance. The police!'

Dad got on the phone.

Coco and Louis rushed over to Madame Auguste. She was still alive. Just. But her breathing was slow and raspy.

'It *is* deadly nightshade!' cried Louis, horrified. 'That must be why he went to the woods.'

Coco felt sick. First Monsieur Framboise, now Madame Auguste!

She gripped Madame Auguste's hand.

Louis took the other.

Belle whined and lay down at her side.

'Madame Auguste, don't worry, we're here,' cried Coco. 'Dad's calling an ambulance.'

But Madame Auguste's eyes just rolled towards the ceiling, and she smiled. 'No need, *ma chère enfant*. Isidore, *j'arrive*! I'm coming.' And then she went limp.

Coco didn't know what to do.

'I think she is dead!' said Louis, shocked.

Mum rushed over to check her pulse, then hung her head.

Then rage filled Coco, erupting like a volcano.

How dare Carmichael do this?!

How dare he trick us?!

Use us?!

How dare he take away people's lives?!

And all for what?

A bunch of silly old recipes!

They needed to stop him!

'He is running back to the hotell!' cried Louis, looking out through the front door.

In a burst of shock and fury, everyone dashed outside. Nothing more could be done for Madame Auguste, but they could still stop Carmichael! And Coco and Louis could guess where he was heading.

34

Sure enough, they stumbled into the lobby to find the wine cellar door wide open – a loud banging noise coming from below.

Belle stood at the top of the stairs, growling.

Coco and Louis peered down to see Carmichael standing among the wine boxes, bashing at the wine cupboard with something shiny . . .

'Look, he has taken the trophy of Monsieur Framboise!' Louis whispered.

And Carmichael didn't even seem worried that they'd followed him. He just turned with a mocking smile and said, 'Oh, good. I always did like an audience!'

Coco felt dazed and frantic in equal measure, as if she were living a nightmare.

'You killed her. You killed her!' Mum cried. She

was hysterical!'

'Oh, so the old dear died?' came the callous reply. 'I hoped she might. How convenient!'

His theatrical voice – so familiar from *Bake the Day* – was now cold and murderous, and it chilled Coco to the very core.

Mum got out her phone. 'The world needs to know who Atticus Carmichael really is!' she whispered. 'I'm going to film everything until the police get here.'

Then, with one last mighty whack, Carmichael broke the back panel and dashed down the stairs into the workshop.

'After him!' shouted Dad, then . . . 'Wait – the wine cupboard really is a door, like Coco said? Are you getting this, Cheryl?'

When they burst into the workshop, Monsieur Framboise was floating in mid-air, just above his worktable.

'Hello, Isidore,' said Carmichael. He didn't even seem surprised to see his victim as a ghost. 'I should have known you'd hang around. You haven't aged a bit. But then again, how could you?' He laughed. And it was a hollow laugh.

'I should have known you'd come back, Nibby,' said Monsieur Framboise. 'You always were sniffing around the wine cellar!'

Mum and Dad stood still as statues, mouths gaping.

'M-Monsieur Framboise i-is REAL!' Mum managed to splutter, her telephone wobbling as her hand trembled.

'And there *is* a workshop in the house!' said Dad.

'Yes!' said Coco. 'That's what I tried to tell you! You wouldn't believe me.'

But this was no time for an argument; they were in too much danger.

'Well,' Carmichael grinned. He had moved over to the cooker and was standing as though on TV – bowtie straight, mouth smiling, like a star playing to the cameras. 'The show's almost over.'

Belle growled at him.

'No, Belle, you mustn't,' said Coco, holding her back. 'I can't risk you getting hurt!'

'My little BBC ruse fooled you for a while,' Carmichael continued. 'But I suppose you're wondering why I'm here?'

'We know why!' cried Coco. 'To steal Monsieur Framboise's recipes.'

'Oh, you're good! Yes! That's right.' Then he turned to the ghost. 'It's all your fault I came back, Isidore.'

'Mine?' Monsieur Framboise bristled at the accusation, a white, angry mist seeping out from under his hat.

'Oh, yes. You see, you died too soon! My plan was to feed you those chocolate berries *after* you'd told me where you kept the recipe cards. But you had to go and eat them all before I got it out of you.'

Sweat was rolling down Carmichael's face now.

'But life went on . . . well, for me, at least. Ha! I kept the Nibby's factory, but changed my name to Atticus Carmichael. More showbiz-like. Plus, I didn't want to be traced back to you, did I? Then I became famous. Blah-blah-blah! Everything I wanted fell into my lap . . . except your recipes!' He spat the last few words.

'Then I saw your post, Cheryl . . .' He said it with that strange uneven smile Coco had seen creeping up his cheek before. 'About the "Chocolatier" sign, and I couldn't resist. I watched all your silly videos. And they made me think – if you were ripping this place apart, maybe, just maybe, you would find Isidore's cards. And so, I came with my BBC story. And you believed it. You invited me in. And then you, children' – his piercing glare burnt through Coco and Louis – 'made the chocolates. And they were magical. Just like in Isidore's day. And I knew the cards were here, somewhere.'

'B-but why kill for recipes?' said Mum, making sure Carmichael couldn't see her phone. 'You're a chef. You can make your own! You've got everything! Restaurants, cookbooks, *Bake the Day*. That's a massive show. You should be happy!'

'Ah, but alas! I am not. You've tasted *his* chocolate.' He spat the word 'his' as he pointed at Monsieur Framboise.

'It is inimitable. The best. Mine? Not so much.'

Of course it isn't! Coco wanted to shout. *Monsieur Framboise's magic ingredient is love, but you're a . . . a monster!* But she was too scared to say it aloud.

'You never could accept it, could you, Nibby?' said Monsieur Framboise. 'You had to be the best at everything.'

'Ah, but who's got your trophy now, Isidore?' said Carmichael, brandishing the now bashed-in cup. 'Give me your recipes.' His hand reached out to the cooker and turned on the gas. 'Or I burn the place down!' He held up a lighter.

'No!' shouted Mum and Dad.

The eggy scent of gas filled the air.

'A-WOO-WOO-WOO!' went Belle.

Coco felt dizzy with fear and clung to Louis.

As for Monsieur Framboise, he looked frightened for the first time since Carmichael had arrived. He immediately used his other-worldly powers to conjure a copper saucepan from the wall and place it in a groove in the worktable. Then, he twisted it clockwise to open a panel, which popped up like a trapdoor to reveal . . .

'My recipe book,' he said, holding it lovingly, as if for one last time.

'Don't do it!' cried Coco.

Monsieur Framboise just shook his head. '*Non*. I am

dead, I cannot die again. But you are all alive. You have your whole lives to live. I will not let this man take what is most precious from you – and precious to me, now, too.'

He smiled at the children. 'Recipes are just recipes. But life! That is what's real – what is priceless. Take it, Nib—!'

But Carmichael had already snatched it from his ghostly hand.

'Wonderfully put, Isidore. But it's time to go!' Carmichael announced with a sneer, holding the lighter out in front of him. 'Say farewell to those "*priceless* lives"! Ha!' And with a snap of his thumb he sparked the lighter.

WHOOF!

A fireball from the gas cooker whooshed into the air, narrowly missing Carmichael but catching the wooden shelves by the workshop door. They lit up like giant kindling, sending billows of fire and smoke around the room.

'GET OUT!' cried Mum and Dad.

Monsieur Framboise swooped down to turn off the gas – but it was too late. The flames had already caught on and they were spreading fast . . .

Across the cupboards below the work surface . . .

Into his beloved pantry . . .

Along the wooden wall panels above the tiles.

'Out of my way! Out of my way!' Carmichael pushed past Mum to head for the staircase, but . . .

CRASH!

A shelf fell off the wall and blocked the exit.

Carmichael had been caught out by the rapid spread of his own murderous plan. He was trapped.

They were all trapped.

Coco and Louis covered their mouths with their T-shirts.

Mum and Dad covered their mouths, too. Poor Belle could only howl.

The smoke was suffocating.

And the heat. Oh, the heat!

In the next instant, a mighty flame caused another shelf to fall and then another – like burning dominoes.

Soon, the air was so thick – like black tar – Coco couldn't see or breathe. She had no idea where Louis or Belle, or Mum and Dad were.

She fell to the floor, gasping for air.

This is it! she thought. *Maybe we'll all die and turn into ghosts?*

And that's when it came! A wind so cold that it pushed away the smoke and extinguished part of the fire. It was as if someone had opened a giant freezer. And there, whooshing around the room, making that icy wind, was . . .

'Madame Auguste?' Coco's voice was but a hoarse whisper.

'Madeleine?' cried Monsieur Framboise, his eyes wide

and unbelieving as her body flitted past him in an iridescent glow.

But there was no time for reunions. He understood what she was doing. And she knew he'd understood. And so she held out her hand for him to take. Then together, they whooshed over every flame, pushed back every swirl of smoke and sent the temperature plummeting with their wonderful, deathly coldness.

Coco heaved air into her lungs.

She could see Carmichael, not far away, staring, mesmerized by the spectacle of his victims' ghostly powers.

Until he snapped out of it. And made for the stairs again.

But Monsieur Framboise was one step ahead. 'Belle, now!' he cried.

And off Belle dashed to the staircase, jumping over the fallen shelf to grab Carmichael's trouser leg and pull him back with such force that . . .

'ARGH!' Carmichael screamed as he flew backwards through the air to land with an 'OOF' next to Coco, who was still lying on the floor, blurry-eyed and trying to catch her breath.

But it wasn't over yet . . .

35

Coco could hear the squeal of approaching police sirens, faint at first, then getting louder.

'You're finished, Atticus,' said Dad from somewhere behind her, his voice hoarse from all the smoke.

Coco tried to turn to see where he and Mum were – the fire had been so disorientating – but her head felt too woozy to move, as if her skull might split in two.

'I doubt that, Burt!' came Carmichael's cold, caustic reply. 'I always get a rerun!'

'This isn't TV, you idiot!' Dad retorted. Coco had never heard him so angry.

'No,' Carmichael replied coolly. 'But to quote William Shakespeare – or perhaps it was just my gran – *Pick a fight and run away, you'll live to fight another day!* So toodle-oo!' He bowed theatrically, just like on *Bake the*

Day, then was back on the stairs.

Not for long.

Loud shouting in French echoed down: '*Police! Vous êtes en état d'arrestation!*' And not a second later, there was Carmichael again, struggling against two police officers.

'Get off me, you animals!' he screamed, as more footsteps resounded on the stairs above.

Then as the police forced Carmichael's wrists into handcuffs, Coco saw the recipe book drop to the floor and land . . . by her feet.

Forcing herself to move despite her headache, she stretched out a foot and pushed the book up towards her hand and . . . *just a bit further* . . . grasped it tightly to her chest. Phew! It was safe.

As for Carmichael, he kicked at the officers' legs. But it was no good. He was well and truly caught.

'I'll sue you all! You can't do this to me! I'm famous!' he wailed.

'Infamous, you mean,' said Mum, victoriously. 'I got it! I filmed it all. Now everyone will see what you've done!'

'Why you—'

'Save it for your lawyer, *monsieur*!' said the officer on the left, cutting him off, before turning to address the room. 'Stay here, everyone. We will come back to help!' And off they went with Carmichael, for good this time.

'NOOOOOO!' His desperate and deranged roar echoed above as he realized he'd lost the recipes, he was under arrest and the truth was finally out!

Perhaps it was the emotion?

Perhaps it was the fire and the smoke?

Probably, it was all three. But Coco suddenly felt faint, and was relieved when Dad heaved her up into his arms to carry her over to Mum and Belle, who hugged and licked and hugged and licked her (the licking part was from Belle) as though they thought they'd lost her forever. Coco wanted to cry with relief. Her family was safe and she'd got the recipe book. But . . .

'Where's Louis?' she shrieked in panic, looking around, realizing she'd not heard his voice for a while.

'Here!' came Louis's hoarse whisper.

Relief washed over Coco like warm water.

'With us!' his mum and dad said together.

'We came down behind the police,' said his mum. 'We heard the sirens, saw the smoke . . .' Her voice petered out with emotion.

So, it was his parents' footsteps she'd heard on the steps behind the police.

Then everyone huddled together, taking everything in: the black, charred workshop; the grimy, cracked tiles; the brittle, burnt cupboards. Only the copper pots seemed to have withstood the flames – though they'd lost their shine.

But none of it mattered, because they were alive.

Thanks to the ghosts.

The ghosts! Coco gasped, suddenly panicked. Where were they?

It was Belle who sensed them first, whining as she stared at nothing in the vaulted ceiling.

Then suddenly, there were Monsieur Framboise and Madame Auguste floating down through the stonework towards the ground.

And as they touched the floor, a glorious, sparkling light – like a sunbeam laced with stars and rainbows – illuminated their bodies from above. And it seemed to be coming from somewhere beyond the *oubliette* ceiling – a dimension outside this earth.

Coco felt tears in her eyes. She'd never seen anything so beautiful.

'*F-fantômes!*' cried Louis's parents, suddenly realizing that their son had been right about the hotel all along.

'Look at Madame Auguste!' cried Louis.

Coco turned to see that their late neighbour was now young again – long-haired and beautiful, just as she had been when Monsieur Framboise died. And Monsieur Framboise was glowing – quite literally, as bright as a lightbulb.

'Coco!' cried Louis. 'I think we finally know what

Monsieur Framboise's unfinished business was. Being with Madeleine again!'

Oh no. This is it. For real, thought Coco. *Monsieur Framboise is going to leave.* Part of her felt happy, for him and Madame Auguste. But the other part thought her heart would break. She'd never see him again!

A quiet fell in the workshop as everyone watched on, wondering what would happen next. Even Belle cocked her head to one side.

'I think it is time to say goodbye,' said Monsieur Framboise. His voice was already distant, as though talking from inside a tunnel.

Coco's heart skipped a beat.

'Unless' – he turned to Madame Auguste in a shower of sparkles – 'you would care to stay here to make *chocolat*, with me?'

Epilogue

As summer faded to autumn and winter warmed to spring, Coco watched the lavender fields around Mont-Lavande transform from purple to silver to brown to green – *Like a moving postcard*, she thought. But that was nothing compared to the changes in her own life.

You see, in the six months since 'Carmichael-gate' (the name the news had given to Carmichael's murderous rampage and his subsequent and unsurprising firing from *Bake the Day*), so many things were different, it was hard to know where to start.

The famous TV chef was now serving a life sentence in prison and wasn't allowed to work in the prison kitchens for fear that he'd poison the other inmates. 'Double punishment for a cook!' Dad had said with satisfaction one morning, as he fixed a brand-new vintage mirror to the lobby wall .

Coco had started French school, which had been hard at first. She'd not understood a word, but little by little, with Louis's help and lots of practice in class and at home, she could now follow her lessons and – Mum said – speak French rather well.

She still made silly mistakes – like when she'd wanted to ask Louis why he looked sad, one day, but said '*Tu as l'air truite!*' which means, 'You look like a trout' (*triste* means 'sad', *truite* is 'trout'); and when she'd wanted to tell a girl in her class that she liked her new haircut, but said '*J'aime ton cheval!*', which means 'I like your horse' (*cheval* is 'horse', *cheveux* is 'hair') – but now she saw the funny side.

Plus, despite her worries and mistakes, she'd not had any trouble making new friends, as all the children already knew who she was through Carmichael-gate, and frequently came to ask her for help with their English homework!

Her newest and closest friend (after Louis), though, was Romy, and if the name sounds familiar, it should. She was the girl who'd asked for their photo on the square, remember? She was in the year above Coco and Louis at school, but had walked straight over to them on the first day of term and they'd gelled like chocolate and cream ever since.

Coco still missed Kate and Rose a lot. She still hadn't seen them since she'd left England. But with Louis and Romy as her friends, she wasn't lonely any more. Romy (who lived in Ville-Verte) came over most Saturdays to hang out at the hotel and – though shocked at first to discover it was haunted – now loved the ghosts just as much as Coco and Louis.

For yes, Monsieur Framboise and Madame Auguste had decided to stay!

Madame Auguste had even decided to move into the hotel permanently – something she and Monsieur Framboise had announced just after her funeral, as the Beans held a memorial party for her in the kitchen (just themselves and the ghosts).

Coco thought it must be strange attending your own death celebration, but Madame Auguste had seemed to enjoy it.

As Monsieur Framboise brought out trays of 'Chococrypte' – dark, gravestone-shaped chocolates, laced with popping candy (which, he said, reminded him of the tickly afterlife light he and Madame Auguste had been bathed in) – Madame Auguste had kissed him and cried, 'Together forever, Isidore!'

But no one was as happy as Mum and Dad.

Carmichael-gate, though tragic, had turned Mum into a bit of a star. She now had more followers than she could count, and had made enough money to pay off their big bank loan.

The attention had even drawn more people to the village, and some had decided to move in. For every boarded-up building before, now there were . . .

Here, let's take a tour:
- A butcher's, next to the bakery
- A florist's, next to Café de la Poste
- A grocer's on the main square, next to . . .
- The brand-new Café Mont-Lavande, whose tables were set around the fountain
- A bike repair shop, by the church

and even
- A perfume shop in the house next door to Madame Auguste's old one

The money had allowed Dad to finish the entire hotel too, and the first guests were set to arrive tonight for . . . you guessed it . . . an Easter celebration!

But not just any Easter celebration.

The Hôtel Framboise Easter Launch Party!

Their French dream had come true.

The hotel was officially open!

'*Attention aux œufs*, Monsieur Framboise!' Coco said, as the ghost floated up the new, fire-proofed chocolate workshop stairs with a pile of Easter eggs wobbling on a silvery tray.

'I made the eggs, Coco!' he snapped back. 'Of course I will be careful! *Pfff!*' He turned to Madame Auguste, who was floating behind him with a collection of chocolate bunnies. 'I think I liked her more when she only spoke English. Less bossy!' He grinned.

'You ignore him!' laughed Madame Auguste, sweeping across the new black-and-white chequerboard lobby floor.

'Coming through,' cried Louis. He was carrying a tall pile of handmade Easter egg boxes to the new shop – all dark wood, marble and brass set in a corner of the lobby – where Dad, Romy and the ghosts were about to create an Easter display. There were to be:

- Chocolate eggs and bunnies
- Caramel Stars (the Hôtel Framboise version)
- Madeleines (buttery little sponge cakes) dipped in chocolate (in honour of Madame Auguste)
- Belle Bites, special dog-safe chocolate cups that Monsieur Framboise had invented with carob – not chocolate – and peanut butter

'Made with love for you, my sweet,' he said, picking one off the display and handing it to Belle, who wolfed it down.

And ...

- Choco-Chéris (cherry fondant in white chocolate), Rêves Cacao (dreamy chocolate truffles), Coeurs

Fondants (gooey praline-filled heart shapes), Bijou Bonbons (jewel-shaped chocolate drops filled with raspberry ganache), Mini-Mousses (little cups of milk chocolate mousse) and every other chocolate from Monsieur Framboise's recipe book, now safe and sound again – thanks to Coco – in a new hiding place

'Coco, can you go outside and set up some tables?' called Mum from their now-fancy kitchen. 'Louis's parents need one for their jam stand, Madame Tiffet's bringing food and Monsieur Dubois will be here any second with the drinks.'

'*Oui!*' called Coco, stepping out.

She looked around. The new cafe owners had strung bright-pink bunting up along Café Mont-Lavande's old stone facade for the party. Dad had filled the hotel's window boxes with tufty raspberry-coloured flowers, and Mum had put fairy lights up in the trees by the fountain, above where the tables would be set. It looked so pretty. Just the sort of thing Kate and Rose would have liked.

Her thoughts turned to her friends back in England. What a shame they couldn't be there. She hadn't seen them for . . . she sighed . . . forever.

Coco's phone pinged. She took it from her pocket. And as if on cue . . .

KATE

Thinking of you today. Hope you have fun!

ROSE

Yeah! Sorry we can't be there ☹

Coco felt a lump in her throat.

KATE

Just kidding – turn around.

'What?' Coco swung around.

There, walking with their families across the far side of the light-dappled square, were Kate and Rose!

'WHA—? HOW?' Coco's heart raced with shock.

'Surprise!' called Mum and Dad from the front step. Monsieur Framboise and Madame Auguste were floating above them, waving.

Louis, Romy and Belle immediately rushed over to Coco.

'Were you all in on this?' she said in disbelief. She wanted to cry.

'Of course!' said Louis.

Belle barked.

And before she knew it, Coco was hugging Kate and Rose, and introducing Louis and Romy, and they were chatting and laughing, and it was just like old times.

And in that moment, she knew.

Life at Hôtel Framboise was going to be sweet!

BAISERS AU CHOCOLAT
(Chocolate Kisses)

INGREDIENTS

- 170g milk chocolate
- 60g raspberry jam, seedless if preferred

EQUIPMENT

- Bain-marie (saucepan and bowl)
- Chocolate mould (oval shaped, 10 to 12 chocolates, approximately 5cm x 3cm)
- Pastry brush or other food-safe brush

Make sure you get a grown-up to help you, especially with the bain-marie, as the hot water is dangerous.

METHOD

1) Melt the milk chocolate in a bain-marie

2) Use the brush to dab a thin coat of chocolate around the mould, then cool in the fridge for five minutes

3) Repeat step 2 another four times

4) Fill each shell with a dollop of raspberry jam

5) Pour a layer of the chocolate on top to seal the chocolates, then cool again

6) Remove from the mould

Acknowledgements

It's a strange thing, writing a book. You spend hours alone with just your words and your thoughts, then suddenly you're part of a team. And what a team!

Thank you to everyone at Chicken House: my fantabulous editor and publisher Rachel Leyshon, Barry Cunningham (publishing icon), Laura Myers, Esther Waller, Fraser Crichton and Rachel Hickman, along with Ruth Kenyon, Jazz Bartlett Love, Elinor Bagenal, Laura Smythe, Mark Ecob and everyone else who has worked so hard to get this book out in the world.

It was the hugely talented Emily Jones who drew the cover and all the beautiful inside bits. Emily, Monsieur Framboise is EXACTLY how I imagined! Thank you.

Thank you too to my fellow author friends Annaliese Avery (you are a fountain of fab ideas), Yvonne Banham, Adam Connors, Clare Harlow, Michael Mann and Chrissie Sains.

And to my husband Pascal Chind, my constant through thick and thin.

And to Eric Morlot – without your generosity and patience, I couldn't have done any of it.

And a special thanks to Sam Copeland at RCW. You are an agent *extraordinaire*.

But the BIGGEST thank you goes to you, dear READER. I wrote this book for you, so thank you for picking it up.

Why not drop me an email at annabrookewriter@gmail.com (just be sure to have permission from a parent or guardian first) to tell me what you thought of it, and, if you make Monsieur

Framboise's recipe, send me some pictures of the chocolates. I'd love to see how they turn out.

Tell your teacher I'm open to school visits too. There's nothing nicer than talking all things books in classrooms.

Meanwhile, if you'd like to find out more about me and other books I've written, go to my website: annabrookewriter.com. There will be another *Coco Bean Investigates* book along soon, so get ready for more mystery!

With love,
Anna

P.S. Coco's cocker spaniel was inspired by my very own dog, Belle. Here's a photo.